Trouble in Paradise

I couldn't think of a more exciting way to spend a week. Once I got used to the bumpiness of the ride, I slipped into a daydream, imagining myself traipsing through the rain forest, surrounded by all types of exotic animals.

The rest of the journey passed quickly, and soon the taxi came to an abrupt halt in front of Corcovado Ecologica.

The place looked nothing like what I'd imagined. The minute I took in the scene, I felt a horrible sinking feeling in the pit of my stomach. Something was seriously wrong.

NANCY DREW
girl detective™

#1 Without a Trace
#2 A Race Against Time
#3 False Notes
#4 High Risk

#5 Lights, Camera . . .
#6 Action!
#7 The Stolen Relic
#8 The Scarlet Macaw Scandal

Available from Aladdin Paperbacks

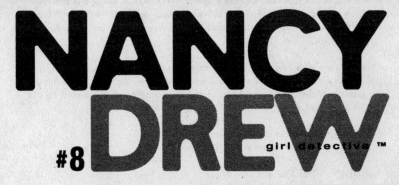

NANCY DREW
girl detective ™
#8

The Scarlet Macaw Scandal

CAROLYN KEENE

Aladdin Paperbacks
New York   London   Toronto   Sydney

First Aladdin Paperbacks edition November 2004
Copyright © 2004 by Simon & Schuster, Inc.

ALADDIN PAPERBACKS
An imprint of Simon & Schuster
Children's Publishing Division
1230 Avenue of the Americas
New York, NY 10020

Manufactured in the United States of America
10   9   8

Library of Congress Control Number 2004101554
ISBN-13: 978-0-689-86844-3
ISBN-10: 0-689-86844-8

Contents

1	*An Auspicious Beginning*	1
2	*A Surprise Visitor*	14
3	*Monkey Madness*	28
4	*Trouble Ahead*	42
5	*Suspicion Grows*	53
6	*Crash Landings*	64
7	*A Rain Forest Romance*	76
8	*Just Dropping In*	82
9	*A Surprising Discovery*	92
10	*The Thief Strikes Again*	100
11	*Ruffled Feathers*	112
12	*The Terrible Truth*	127
13	*Caught!*	138
14	*Another Girl Detective*	146

An Auspicious Beginning

As we touched down on a landing strip only slightly larger than our small plane, Bess squeezed my hand. "Nancy Drew!" she said. "I can't believe we're finally here." Her blue eyes were shining and her smile was even brighter than usual.

I was just as thrilled, of course. How could I not be? Bess, George, and I were about to spend an entire week in a Costa Rican rain forest. We were part of a team of volunteers, studying tourism's effect on wildlife with three scientists from the University of River Heights. "We're going to have the most amazing week," I said as I pulled my strawberry blond hair up into a ponytail.

"Forget about this week," said George. "I'm just thrilled to finally be getting off the plane." As soon as

1

the pilot secured the brakes, George stood up and stretched. "Who knew the trip to Corcovado National Park would take this long?"

Dan Margolis, a tall and handsome environmental scientist, must have overheard George because he kindly corrected her mistake. "Oh, we're not quite there yet."

George raised her eyebrows. "Don't tell me I have to get on another plane," she cried. "This is already the third one today!"

Dan laughed as he shook his head. "No, we only have a taxi ride left."

"A taxi ride," George repeated. "*That* I can deal with. How far is the lodge from here?"

"It's about forty miles away," Dan explained. "But since the only way there is on a narrow, dirt road that cuts through the forest, it'll take us at least two hours."

"Two hours?" Bess asked. She and George exchanged a tired look.

I knew exactly where my friends were coming from. We'd left River Heights many hours ago, and I felt like I'd been traveling for days. Once I stepped off the plane, though, any concern I had about the additional travel time was forgotten. I'd just walked into the middle of paradise!

The deep, blue Pacific Ocean flowed gently on my

2

right, and on my left stood a lush, tropical rain forest. Colorful birds flew overhead, and a stunning beach of soft, white sand stretched for miles down the coast. I breathed in the fresh air and basked in the warmth of the bright, buttery yellow sun. Back in River Heights it was the dead of winter, and I was thrilled to have a week-long break from the cold and snow.

As the rest of the team stepped off the plane, Bess slipped on a pair of sunglasses. "I didn't know it would be this beautiful!" she exclaimed.

Dan pointed to a nearby tree. "Look, everyone," he said. "Someone's watching us."

I glanced up and immediately gasped. Staring down at us from the highest branches of one of the tallest trees were four little monkeys. "Those are white-faced capuchins, right?" I asked.

"Good guess." Dan smiled at me. "You can tell from their coloring, of course. They're the only monkeys in the rain forest that have such distinctive white faces, necks, and chests, in contrast to their dark brown, furry bodies."

"Like a cappuccino," Bess added. "It's got the frothy, white milk on top, and the dark, brown espresso on the bottom."

"Exactly," said Dan, slipping on a pair of aviator sunglasses.

As I pulled out my binoculars to get a closer look,

I realized the monkeys were climbing down to lower branches so they could get a better view of us. I'd never seen anything like it.

"I'm surprised they're not afraid of us," George commented.

The monkeys' behavior reminded me of a passage in the field guide I'd studied in preparation for our trip. "This is natural. I read that the capuchins are curious," I volunteered, "and they're much more likely to be around people than the other types of monkeys found in Costa Rica. Since squirrel monkeys are so rare, they only exist in really isolated areas. I can't imagine finding one near an airport." I smiled to myself, since the so-called airport consisted of a cement landing strip in the middle of the sand, and nothing else.

"That's true, and it's why we aren't going to be studying squirrel monkeys this week," said Dan. "I'm really impressed with your knowledge. But do you know about the other two types of monkeys that are found here?"

"Of course," I replied. I'd done a ton of reading about Costa Rican wildlife in the past few weeks. I would have mentioned the other monkeys before, but I didn't want to sound like a know-it-all. But now that Dan had asked . . .

"Well, there's the mantled howler monkey, which we'd be more likely to hear than see, since their

4

voices can carry from up to a kilometer away, even in a dense rain forest like this one," I said. "And the fourth species found in Costa Rica is the spider monkey. They have long, rail-thin arms and legs, which are very useful for climbing. They're probably the fastest moving monkeys found in Central America. Apparently, to see them swing from tree to tree, you'd think they had wings!"

Dan ran his hand through his thick, blond hair. "You've certainly done your homework," he said.

"She always does," said George, raising her camera and taking a few pictures of the monkeys. "What else would you expect from the famous Nancy Drew?"

Dan's jaw dropped. "You're Nancy Drew, the detective?" he asked. "That's so wild! I've read about you in the *River Heights Bugle.*"

As I nodded I felt my cheeks blush red. Regardless of how often I get recognized, I never get used to it. I'm probably the best-known amateur sleuth in River Heights, but it's not like I set out to earn this reputation. It seems to be the natural consequence of helping people whenever I can. While it *is* true that I sometimes seek mysteries out, it's also the case that there's always something fishy brewing in River Heights—and just as often, mysteries have this funny way of finding me.

George pointed her camera toward Dan, and he

put his arm around me as she snapped a shot.

"I'll want a copy of that one," said Dan.

George grinned, saying, "No problem."

"Careful, George," Bess called. "You're going to run out of film before we even get there."

"It's a digital camera," George replied. "Its memory can hold up to two hundred pictures."

"Of *course* my cousin has a digital camera," Bess said as she giggled. "I should have known!"

Dan looked back and forth between my two friends. "You two are cousins?" he asked.

He wasn't the first person to be surprised by this fact. George is tall and thin, with short, dark hair. She was decked out in her usual sporty clothes. Like all of us—or, I should say, almost all of us—her outfit was pretty wrinkled after a long day of travel. In contrast, Bess is shorter and curvier, with long, blond hair. Her khaki pants and pink, cotton shirt seemed as if they'd just been pressed. George looked ready for a hike, and Bess looked like she was about to pose for a magazine spread.

Just because Bess is into fashion does not mean she's a flake, though. She has this amazing mechanical mind, and can fix any type of engine or motor blindfolded and with one hand tied behind her back. It's a talent that's come in handy to me more than once when I've been on a case.

6

Once our baggage was unloaded from the plane, the head scientist, Parminder Patel, cupped her hands around her mouth and shouted to the entire group. "Please get your packs and meet me by that large boulder. The taxis should be here momentarily."

Parminder and I had gotten to know each other that morning when we sat together on our first plane trip of the day. The pretty scientist, with shoulder-length dark hair and large brown eyes, was born in India and raised in North London. That's why she had a British accent. She moved to River Heights to head the science department at the university ten years ago. A passionate environmentalist, she was the first person to conduct research at Corcovado Eco-logica.

I heaved my pack onto my back and went over to say hello.

"Hi, Nancy," said Parminder. "How are you doing?"

"Really great," I replied. "And I'm totally thrilled to be here, of course!"

When Parminder smiled at me, her entire face lit up. "Just wait until you get to the lodge. It's lovely. This is my tenth year visiting, but I can never get enough of the place. The flora and fauna will knock your socks off." Parminder motioned to an old truck that rattled toward us. Its heavy tires kicked up a huge amount of dust, which lingered in its wake like a thick storm cloud. "Splendid!" she said. "Here's the first taxi, right on schedule."

This taxi was like none I'd ever seen. It was a pickup truck with narrow wooden benches lining either side of the flatbed in back. Parminder climbed right on up, and was followed by Mary Wu, the third scientist. It was strange that I hadn't met Mary before the trip, since she was born and raised in River Heights, and her parents own my favorite Chinese restaurant. She had her father's warm and open smile, and she would have had her mother's thick, beautiful black hair, except she'd dyed hers purple. Mary was wearing ripped jeans and a black tank top that read, THE KITCHENETTES. Apparently they're some new, cutting-edge band based in Toronto. I'd never heard of them but Mary let me listen to a couple of their songs on the flight, and they'd sounded pretty good.

Four other volunteers climbed into the taxi. Their names were Stephanie, Kara, Elise, and Benita, and they all belonged to the same University of River Heights sorority, Kappa Delta Theta.

"Since we're twelve people, we'll have to split up into two groups," said Parminder. "We've room for one more in here, though."

"I'll go with Nancy," said Dan.

"Me too," Bess added. "I'd rather wait for a regular taxi, if that's okay. These open-air ones would do horrible things to my hair."

Mary giggled. "Bess, we're in the rain forest now, remember? This *is* a regular taxi."

"Oh," said Bess. Although momentarily stunned, she recovered quickly. Reaching into her purse, she pulled out a pink silk scarf to tie around her head. When the second taxi, identical to the first, pulled up moments later, she was the first to climb in.

Dan got in after Bess, and was followed by George, then Bud and Cathy Reisling. After our introductions, I learned that Bud was a freelance photographer, and Cathy taught philosophy at the university. They'd traveled to many countries, but this was their first time in Costa Rica. Besides helping out with research, Bud planned to take lots of pictures of rain forest animals.

When George heard this, her ears pricked up. She and Bud immediately began comparing their digital cameras and various lenses.

As we traveled down the narrow dirt road, we felt every single bump. We had to duck whenever the taxi drove under low-hanging branches. And let me tell you, there were *lots* of bumps and even *more* low-hanging branches. I held on tightly to the sides of the truck as we rumbled along.

Despite the less-than-comfortable ride, it was a thrilling experience. The thick trees created a canopy, under which the air was clean and damp. Over the roar of the truck I heard mysterious chirping and humming coming from the rain forest's many wild animals. Even though we followed a clearly defined dirt road, ours were the only two vehicles driving on it. I felt as if we were miles away from civilization, exploring brand-new, uncharted territory.

After about an hour had passed, George pulled her laptop computer out of her backpack.

"What are you doing?" Bess asked, raising her voice to be heard over the low rumble of the truck's engine.

"I barely had time to install my Spanish-English translation software before we left," George explained.

"*Hola* means 'hello,'" Bess teased. "That was off the top of my head. I didn't need to take my computer all the way to the rain forest to know that!"

"Well, it's a good thing," George countered, pointing to Bess's things. "Because with all of the clothes you brought, you'd have no room for a computer— or anything else practical—in your bag!"

Bess sat up straighter. "As we all know, our research will involve hiking through the rain forest and observing and counting monkeys. I have my hiking boots and my brain. I even brought a notebook and a few pens to record data. What else do I need?"

George, the biggest technology buff I know, ticked off her list of necessities on the fingers of one hand. "A digital camera, a computer to record and organize the data, a portable global positioning system—you know, a GPS—so you know where you are, and if you don't have that, then a compass. I prefer digital models, though, because they're much more accurate. And I could go on."

Bess faked a yawn. "Please don't. I slept enough on the plane."

Looking back and forth between them, Dan laughed. "Are you two always like this?"

"Nah," said George, wiggling her eyebrows. "We're just getting started!"

Everyone in the taxi burst into laughter.

"Between the crazy cousins and the famous detective—with the prettiest blue eyes I've ever seen—I have a feeling this week is going to be fantastic," said Dan.

Suddenly feeling a little flustered, I stared down at my feet. "Most people just call me Nancy," I said softly.

"Okay, then," Dan replied. "Nancy it is."

"So, tell me more about Corcovado National Park." I was genuinely curious, but I also wanted to change the subject. "You've been here before, right?"

Dan nodded. "It's my fifth time here. I'm not a full professor yet, like Mary and Parminder—I'm still finishing up my degree. These trips are part of my research. Even if it weren't for school, though, I would still come. The lodge is amazing. It's miles away from any town or village, yet it's so well run. Everyone there is very careful about respecting the environment. The lights are solar powered, and the staff recycles almost everything. And even though the place is always booked to capacity, with people visiting from all over the world, it's completely serene. The land is so vast, it's possible to go on a hike and feel like you're the only person in the universe."

"Sounds amazing," I said. "Do you think we'll spot all four types of monkeys at the park?"

"I can't say for sure," said Dan. "As you know, those squirrel monkeys are tricky. You'll definitely see the other three types during your research. And of course, there are also armadillos, butterflies, iguanas, and frogs. If you look carefully, it's possible to spot sloths. They're hard to see because, true to their name, they don't move around too much, so they blend in with the scenery. Oh—how could I forget the tropical birds? They're incredible!"

I couldn't think of a more exciting way to spend a week. Once I got used to the bumpiness of the ride,

I slipped into a daydream, imagining myself traipsing through the rain forest, surrounded by all types of exotic animals.

The rest of the journey passed quickly, and soon the taxi came to an abrupt halt in front of Corcovado Ecologica.

The place looked nothing like what I'd imagined. The minute I took in the scene, I felt a horrible sinking feeling in the pit of my stomach. Something was seriously wrong.

2

A Surprise Visitor

It sounds strange, but when it comes to sensing trouble, I have sort of a sixth sense. I don't really know where it came from or how I got it, but at the moment, I could only focus on one thing: As soon as the taxi stopped, I sensed that something was awry.

It wasn't just the fact that Dan, Mary, and Parminder were speechless. It was the resort. We'd come to Corcovado Ecologica Lodge expecting to find a jungle paradise, but had arrived to find the place in a total shambles.

The wooden WELCOME sign was split in two jagged pieces. Each bit hung to its post by one rusty nail, creaking noisily as it swayed in the breeze. Bare, dirty mattresses stood in a pile out front, and fallen trees blocked the entrance. As we stepped over the mess, Mary knelt by a pile of mud. "This used to be the vegetable garden," she said sadly.

Parminder pointed to a group of rocks. "And that's where the fresh herbs were."

Dazed, we stood in an open area under a thatched roof that was held up by four wooden posts. Dan explained that it was once a lounge filled with hammocks, couches, and colorful cushions. "It was a great space. Every evening we'd gather here to sip mango and papaya juice and watch the sunset," he said. "I can't understand why it's now a dump!"

Suddenly a tall, blond, heavy-set man approached. After mumbling something into a walkie-talkie, he turned to us. "So the River Heights group returns?" he asked gruffly. "I'm the resort manager."

"Hello, Jason," said Parminder, extending her hand. "I remember you. Lovely to see you again. You know Dan Margolis and Mary Wu from past trips, but please allow me to introduce you to our new volunteers. This is—"

Jason cut her off. "Here's where you'll be sleeping." He pointed to the mess of nearly collapsed tents in the distance. "There's room for four in each one, and things aren't exactly busy here, so you'll have plenty of tents to choose from. We didn't have time to get them ready, but we are in the jungle, so I'm sure that none of you were expecting luxury." He glanced at me.

"Excuse me, Jason," said Parminder. "Do you happen to know where Esteban Garcia is?"

"He quit." Jason turned to walk away.

"Surely you're mistaken," Parminder called after him. Her voice was strained when she added, "I don't understand how—"

"Neither do I," Jason replied sharply, interrupting her again. "He just walked out of here last week, leaving me completely in the lurch."

"But I just spoke to him," Parminder went on. "He didn't tell me he was having any problems here."

"Yeah, well, I'm as surprised as you are," said Jason.

"I doubt that," Parminder replied under her breath.

Jason glanced at his watch impatiently. "Dinner will be served in half an hour, with or without you, so I suggest you get a move on." Spinning on his heel, he took off.

"Are you thinking what I'm thinking?" Bess asked in a low voice as we followed the bewildered group through the mess.

"If you're thinking that we may *already* have a new mystery to solve, then yes," I whispered back, keeping my eyes on Parminder. She looked like she was close to tears, and I had to find out why. "Why don't you and George find a tent for the three of us? I'm going to talk to Parminder for a little while."

"Sounds like a plan," Bess said with a nod. "Good luck."

"Thanks," I replied.

The rest of the group wandered off toward the tents, but Parminder hung back, so I did too. She leaned against one of the posts that held up the thatched roof, staring at the mess. Her shoulders were slumped, and if her hair hadn't been moving in the breeze, I might have mistaken her for a statue in a wax museum—a totally depressed statue.

"Parminder, are you okay?" I asked carefully.

She turned to me and blinked, sighing deeply before answering. "Yes, of course. I'm fine—just a little surprised, I suppose."

"Why is that?"

Parminder rubbed her eyes tiredly. "Esteban Garcia, the man I asked Jason about . . . He was the resident biologist here. I just spoke to him two weeks ago, and he said nothing about leaving."

"Do you think he would have told you?" I asked.

The head scientist nodded gravely. "I'm sure of it. Or at least, I used to be."

I sensed that something else was bothering Parminder. Even though I didn't want to pry, I had the feeling that she had information that could be useful. "He was a friend of yours?"

"You could say that," Parminder explained. "We'd

known each other for a long time. I've been coming here for ten years, and Esteban has lived here for even longer than that. As you know, this part of Costa Rica is very remote. He's one of the few people who comes from Corcovado and has stayed here. Most families move away to find work in the cities or larger towns. But Esteban has always been very involved in preservation work at the lodge. He loves the rain forest, and he's very dedicated to protecting his homeland. It doesn't make any sense that he would leave so abruptly, especially without telling me."

"That does seem odd," I agreed, wanting to know more. "You said you just spoke to him, and he didn't mention anything. Would there be any reason for him not to tell you?"

Before Parminder could say anything further, a piercing scream ripped through the air. It came from the tent area.

"Oh, dear!" cried Parminder as we both ran toward the sound.

I was out of breath by the time I made it to the tents. Once there, I looked around to see where the noise had come from—but the only thing I saw was a very sheepish Bess standing beside a large, blue canvas tent.

"What happened?" I asked.

18

"Nothing," Bess chirped.

"Nothing?" Parminder repeated, looking around. "Didn't you hear that scream?"

Other team members were cautiously approaching.

"Oh, that," said Bess. "It was me. It's okay, though! I'm sorry everyone. It's nothing." She tucked a strand of hair behind her ear as she looked at the ground, her face turning beet red. "I just got, um, startled."

"I don't understand," Parminder said.

Bess started to giggle. "It was something I found on the bed. I wasn't scared—just surprised, because it was so big." She pulled back the opening flap of the tent so we could peer inside.

My reaction wasn't as dramatic as Bess's, but I still jumped when I saw a gigantic green bullfrog sitting in the middle of the bed.

"We don't have those big, fat, warty types in River Heights," Bess explained, as she gently shooed the frog out of the tent.

"Welcome to the rain forest," Parminder said to Bess. Then turning to the crowd that had gathered round, she announced, "Nothing to worry about."

As everyone dispersed, she spoke to me in a low voice. "Thank you for your concern, Nancy, but please don't worry. The mess at the lodge and even Esteban's strange disappearance are both secondary to our purpose here. Tomorrow we'll begin our work, and I'm sure things will pick up from there."

"Are you sure?" I asked. "Because I'd be happy to look into the matter further."

Parminder shook her head. "Please don't worry about it. I'm going to find a tent and get settled before dinner. I'll see you girls soon."

After Parminder left I asked, "Where's George?"

"Right here," George replied, coming up behind me. "I was looking for a place to charge my computer battery. It turns out that the only power outlets in this entire place are in the manager's office. I asked Jason if I could borrow one for a little while, but he said he was too busy." She peered inside the tent. "So, this is where we're staying? It's not what we expected, huh?"

George was right. The tent was spacious, but filthy. It looked like it hadn't been cleaned in months. The three of us did what we could to straighten out the mess, wiping down the mud-streaked mattresses before laying our sleeping bags down, sweeping the dirt back outside where it belonged, and finally, laying out our pillows.

"We'd better hurry," Bess said as she ran a brush through her hair. "Something tells me that Jason wasn't kidding when he said dinner would be served with or without us."

George scrunched up her nose. "That guy gives me the creeps."

I don't believe in judging people so quickly, but I had to admit, Jason was pretty rude. Since he was the manager, I'd have to question him later about the mess, and I wasn't looking forward to it. Based on his initial welcome, I got the feeling that he wasn't going to be friendly. But that's never stopped me from digging for a little information before.

Suddenly a bell rang out. "That must be the signal for dinner," said Bess. "And not a second too soon. I'm starving."

We soon discovered that the dining hall was the only well-kept area at the lodge. Like the lounge area, the hall had a large wooden platform for a floor, and a thatched roof supported by four large posts—no walls. But unlike the lounge area, the dining area was spotless.

A pretty blue tablecloth covered the long picnic table in the center. There were already neat rows of plates and silverware set out on either side. At one end of the table sat four pitchers—two filled with water, and two filled with mango juice. I counted twelve place settings for twelve volunteers. It seemed strange that there was no one else staying at Corcovado Ecologica—it was supposed to be a very popular spot. But then, it wasn't its usual beautiful self.

Dan was already seated and chatting with Bud and Cathy. When he spotted Bess, he waved. "I saved you guys some seats."

While there was definitely something strange going on at the lodge, Dan's behavior was no mystery at all. In River Heights and in other cities and countries we've traveled to, one thing has remained constant—guys always fall for Bess. Not only is she a beauty—with corn-silk hair, a peaches-and-cream complexion, and big blue eyes—she's also an expert flirt.

"*Someone's* got a crush," George whispered.

"No kidding," I said with a laugh. "Just let him down easy, okay, Bess? He's a nice guy."

Bess pulled me aside and asked, "Nancy, are you blind? It's so obvious that Dan has no interest in me!"

"What are you talking about?" I wondered.

"He likes *you*, silly," said George.

"There's no way." I couldn't believe it.

"He *had* to share a taxi with you," Bess reminded me. "And remember when George took your picture? He asked for a copy."

"Well, yeah . . . but he was only being friendly," I argued.

Bess grinned and winked at me. "Yeah. We'll see."

I didn't get where my friends were coming from, but the whole thing didn't really matter anyway. I have a steady boyfriend back home named Ned Nickerson, and we've been together for ages. It's always been hard to think about any other guy, since Ned is so fantastic. He's kind, thoughtful, and smart as a whip. Even though it's not his thing, he's always willing to help me solve mysteries. Plus, he has the cutest dimples!

As we sat down with Dan, a young, beautiful girl with dark skin and bright blue-green eyes came over to our table.

George leaned in, whispering, "This is the perfect chance to use my new translation software." Typing some words into her computer, she waited a moment and then read, verbatim, *"Arroz con pollo, por favor."*

The waitress raised her hand to her mouth and giggled. "You mean you want chicken and rice for dinner?" she asked in flawless English. "I'm so glad, because that's just what we're serving!"

Since George was speechless, the girl introduced herself. "I am Manuela Pesa. Welcome to Corcovado Ecologica."

After we all introduced ourselves, Manuela explained, "Things at this kitchen work a little differently from what you're used to, I think. Everyone eats the same thing at the lodge. You see, usually this place is so crowded, and the kitchen is so small, that it's only possible to prepare one dish. I help out, but we have only one official cook. And she happens to be my mother—so I hope you like the food!"

I didn't know if I'd like the food, but I was sure of one thing—I liked Manuela. She seemed so friendly and outgoing. "I'm sure we will," I told her. "It smells delicious. But listen—can I ask you something? How come it's so empty here now?"

Manuela scanned the nearly empty dining hall. "It's so strange. People stopped coming here a few months ago, when—"

Just then an older woman, with gray-streaked hair pulled into a bun and the same beautiful eyes and dark skin as Manuela, walked up to our table, put her arm around Manuela, and whispered something to her.

I didn't need to speak Spanish to understand that our waitress had just been warned not to say anything more.

Manuela coughed and said, "Everyone, please meet my mother, Lupa." She then went on to introduce every single person at the table to her mother. Amazing!

"Do either of you know where Esteban Garcia went?" I pressed. "I heard he left quite suddenly."

Before Manuela or Lupa could answer me, Jason came over to us. "You ask a lot of questions, hmm?" he said with a sneer.

I could tell from the tone of his voice and by the way he glared down at me that he was hinting for me to mind my own business, but I wasn't intimidated. I sensed he might be hiding something, and I had to know what it was.

"I'm Nancy Drew," I said, holding out my hand.

Jason shook it reluctantly.

"I heard this place used to be teeming with tourists." Staring him squarely in the eye, I asked, "What happened?"

Jason shrugged his shoulders. "Who can tell with tourism? I guess the place just fell out of style."

"And what about the other workers?" I asked.

Jason had a quick answer for that, too. "This place has been so hard to book recently that I had to lay off most of the staff. I couldn't pay them. With few people working here, the place is hard to keep up. But then the few tourists we *do* get are unhappy because of the mess, and they don't come back. It's a vicious cycle."

While his answer explained why the lodge was in such disrepair, I wasn't completely satisfied with it. But before I had time to ask him anything else, he was already heading into his office. Since it was right between the kitchen and the dining area, we all heard the door slam shut behind him.

As if on cue, the food came. As Manuela had

promised, we had chicken and rice—but that wasn't all. Lupa had also prepared a green salad, some corn and beans, fried plantains, and a large fruit salad for dessert.

The food was delicious, so I couldn't help but notice that Parminder, who sat at the head of the table, hardly touched her dinner. She looked too upset to eat. She was obviously sad that Esteban was gone. But was there more to the story? Did she suspect foul play?

Since the scientists had to prepare for tomorrow's data gathering, I didn't get to talk to Parminder after dinner. I wanted to continue investigating, but Jason had disappeared, and Manuela and Lupa were busy with the dishes. When I offered to help them clean up, they waved me away.

Back in our tent, Bess, George, and I played two rounds of cards as I filled them in on what I learned from my earlier talk with Parminder.

"So we have Esteban, the missing biologist; Jason, the cranky manager; and Parminder, the depressed environmental scientist," said George.

"You forgot about the bullfrog," Bess joked. "Clearly, someone is trying to intimidate us!"

As we laughed, I gathered up the cards and asked, "Anyone want to play another hand?"

George yawned. "Not me. I'm too exhausted."

"And we need to wake up extra early," said Bess, smoothing out her pajamas.

"The alarm on my digital watch is set for seven A.M.," George assured us.

"Sounds good to me," I said, crawling into my sleeping bag. It'd never felt so cozy, so it was no surprise that I drifted off to sleep almost as soon as my head hit the pillow.

A few hours after I fell asleep, a strange noise—a loud and vicious bellowing—filled the tent.

My eyes flew open and I shot up. It was too dark to see my hand in front of my face, and my heart felt like it was pumping at a rate of a million beats a second.

Suddenly I heard a rustling noise coming from one corner. Within seconds a bright light filled the tent. It was George with her flashlight beam on the flap to the tent. "What's that noise?" she asked warily.

"I don't know," Bess cried, cupping her hands to her ears. "But I don't like it!"

3

Monkey Madness

Suddenly it hit me what the sound was. "This is completely normal!" I assured my friends.

Bess shot me a look as if she thought I was nuts. "Only if you're in the middle of a horror movie could this be considered normal!" she shouted.

"Those are howler monkeys," I explained, having to raise my voice to be heard. Up until a minute ago, I'd only read about the noise. Experiencing it first-hand was a whole different thing—a whole different, very unsettling thing. "They make those sounds to intimidate their predators."

George shone her flashlight around the tent. "I'm not even a predator, and they're intimidating me," she said.

Cringing at a particularly loud and vicious howl, I had to admit that the noise was very creepy.

Determined to remain calm, I told my friends, "Some other animal must be invading their space. I'm sure the sound'll die down soon."

After a few moments George put her flashlight away, and we all settled back down into our sleeping bags. The howling continued for what seemed like ages. We all tossed and turned for what seemed like hours.

I'm not sure what happened first—if the monkeys stopped bellowing, or if I got used to their horrible sounds. But at some point I must have fallen asleep because the next thing I knew, Bess was shaking my arm. "Nancy? Wake up. You slept through George's alarm and it's already seven thirty. We're supposed to be at breakfast."

"Oh no!" Scrambling out of bed, I slipped on some shoes and hurried to the bathroom, which was in a separate structure about fifty yards from our tent, to wash up.

By the time I made it to the dining hall, all of the other volunteers were already there.

"I'm so sorry I'm late," I said, and I grabbed a piece of toast and some scrambled eggs and fruit.

"Not a problem," said Parminder. "You haven't missed anything yet."

"Would you like some coffee?" Dan asked me. "I was just about to get myself a cup."

"No thanks." I sat down across from Bud and Cathy at the other end of the table. They were wearing matching red baseball caps. "Cute hats."

Bud groaned and informed me, "We don't always wear the same clothes. It's just an unlucky coincidence."

"We didn't bring any others and the sun is so strong," Cathy continued.

"Not a big deal at all," I assured them.

"So, how did you sleep?" asked Cathy.

"Not very well," I had to admit. "Those howler monkeys last night were horrible."

Bud grinned. "It's hard to believe that such a beautiful creature can make such a horrible noise, huh?"

"Have you seen them before?" asked Bess, as she spread a thin layer of apricot jam on her toast.

Cathy swallowed a small sip of orange juice before answering. "Bud and I went on a picture-taking safari in Zimbabwe last year. There were lots of howlers there. I wouldn't call them beautiful, though. They're big and thick necked—sort of intimidating looking, but they're very sweet."

"Sweet?" asked George. "They didn't sound very sweet last night."

Cathy nodded. "They are, though. They eat only leaves and fruit and they rarely fight."

"Zimbabwe must have been amazing," I said.

"It was," said Bud. "I'm actually in the process of organizing a gallery show in River Heights. Many of my pictures from the Africa trip will be on display. Of course, I'm hoping to include some shots from this trip too."

"That sounds so cool," said Bess.

Bud smiled. "Thanks. I'll send you all invitations to the opening, if you're interested."

"Definitely," George replied.

Parminder stood up. "It's about time for our briefing," she said.

I quickly finished my toast and faced Parminder. As the chatter died down, she continued. "We're going to break up into four groups to cover all of the hiking trails in the national park. Normally we'd have one scientist per group, but our fourth scientist for this trip, Maria Romano, got sick and had to stay at home. So I'm afraid we'll have to have one group of volunteers without a scientist."

"We can go on our own," George volunteered. "Nancy, Bess, and I have a lot of experience with hiking and exploring. Plus, I have all the latest in tracking technology here in my backpack." She patted her bag and smiled.

"Thank you, George," said Parminder. "If you're all okay with that, you girls can be your own group."

Bess and I nodded with enthusiasm.

31

"Wonderful. You three can take the Ocean View Trail."

After Parminder assigned the rest of the team members and scientists to trails, she explained what the study involved.

Each group was to hike their trail at three points during the day, leaving at precise times: 8:30 A.M., 11:30 A.M., and 2:30 P.M. We were to search for monkeys, count them, make notes about their specific locations and the times of day, and identify their species as howler, capuchin, or spider.

Mary took over to explain the theory behind the study. "Since monkeys are creatures of habit, they tend to visit the same areas every day at the same time, for years on end. So as long as their patterns remain consistent with those of previous years, we'll know that the presence of the lodge and the tourists that it attracts don't have a negative effect on wildlife here."

I was completely psyched. The last time I saw monkeys was when Ned and I went to the River Heights Zoo. Now, don't get me wrong—the zoo is a great place—but seeing monkeys in the wild was a whole other ball game. I mean, it's like choosing between eating spaghetti at your neighborhood restaurant, or at an outdoor café in Rome overlooking the Trevi Fountain. Which would be more exciting? Italy, definitely!

Mary asked, "Are there any questions?"

Bess raised her hand. "I have one. Where is the data from previous years?"

Smiling widely, Mary shook her head. "That's a very good question, but you'll have to wait until tonight. We don't want to give you that information now because it may bias your findings."

As Lupa and Manuela handed us our packed lunches, snacks, and plenty of fresh water, I noticed that Dan was polishing a strange type of knife. Large and shiny, it curved into the shape of an elongated *C*.

"What's that for?" I asked.

"This machete?" As Dan turned the weapon over in his hand it glinted in the sun. "It's for protection because of all the jaguars in the rain forest. Where's yours?"

I gulped, looking from Bess to George. They seemed just as surprised. What sort of trip had we signed up for? "No one said anything about jaguars," I said, blinking.

Dan flashed me a smile and winked. "Just kidding. There are jaguars in the forest, but they're nocturnal. Plus, they're afraid of people. You've got nothing to worry about."

"I would have been less worried if you hadn't told me they exist here in the first place," George pointed out.

Dan laughed. "The trail I'm taking isn't traveled much, so the brush tends to take over. It's impossible to walk through without cutting it back. This machete has never been used on anything other than plant life, and even then, I use it sparingly. I promise."

Parminder glanced at her watch. "It's almost eight thirty, so I'm going to pass out the maps."

"I have some computer software that'll help everyone record their data," George said, pulling her laptop from her backpack.

"Computer software?" Mary gave Parminder a questioning glance and Parminder shrugged.

George told the group, "I designed a program that'll enable us to compare and contrast information more easily. I made copies on floppy disk and CD-ROM. Who wants what?"

"I don't have my computer on me," said Mary.

"And I hardly had room in my bag for my machete," Dan added.

When no one else said anything, George looked around, stunned. "Does *anyone* have a computer?" When no one answered, she asked, "How are you all going to input your findings?"

"I was thinking I'd use a pen and paper," said Dan. "It's sort of old-fashioned, I know, but it's worked for so many years. . . ."

As some of the team members chuckled, George

looked around, clearly bewildered. "Oh. I guess," she said.

Parminder put her hand on George's shoulder. "I can think of many great uses for your computer. Actually, how would you like to be our official data collector?"

"Okay," said George, cheering up a bit. "That won't be a problem at all."

"I'm glad that's settled," said Parminder. "We'll meet back here at six o'clock tonight. You all should finish up an hour or two before, but please be sure to be out of the rain forest by five thirty or so."

Bess shuddered. "Is that when the jaguars come out?" she asked.

"No," Parminder answered with a small grin. "The sun sets early in the rain forest and it gets too dark to see. I wouldn't want anyone getting lost."

"Please don't worry. We haven't lost anyone to jaguars in a year," Dan joked. When Mary shot him a warning look, he threw up his hands. "Again, kidding. I should probably keep my mouth shut." He grinned.

As the group dispersed, George, Bess, and I headed off to the Ocean View Trail. After climbing a fairly steep hill, I realized why the trail was called Ocean View. From our height we had a clear view of the Pacific. We stopped to catch our breath and watched the beautiful, large waves crashing against the shore.

"It's so hot up here," George observed, wiping the back of her neck with a bandanna.

"But so pretty," said Bess with a sigh.

I had to agree—about the heat *and* the gorgeous views. But we couldn't stay there for very long. We had work to do.

Entering the thick of the forest, we soon found ourselves on a path so narrow we had to walk in single file. I took the lead. Bess followed me, and George trailed far behind, snapping pictures along the way.

The trees were dense and the farther and higher we walked, the darker and colder it got. We had to step carefully, since the ground was soft with mud and many layers of damp leaves.

"This is so amazing," said Bess, admiring some purple orchids at our feet.

George was busy typing something into her computer as she walked.

"We haven't found any monkeys yet, George," I pointed out. "What are you doing?"

"I need to record the exact time that we left," George answered.

"I thought your batteries were running low," said Bess.

"I still have two hours of power left." Suddenly

George tripped over a tree root and stumbled. Luckily she caught her balance before falling or dropping her computer.

"Are you okay?" Bess and I asked.

George grinned sheepishly. "I'm fine. But maybe I'll put this away for a little while."

A few moments later I noticed a flash of color from the corner of my eye. I looked down and saw the most amazing thing: Nestled between two rotting logs sat three tiny frogs. Each was smaller than my thumb, and they had vibrant orange bodies and bright blue legs.

"Wow!" I marveled.

Bess crouched down next to me. "Those are so cute! I wish one of those had ended up in our tent last night instead of that ugly bullfrog!"

George snapped a few shots of the frogs who, probably startled by the flash, darted away. "Oops," said George. "Sorry about that."

"No biggie," I told her.

There were plenty of other frogs in the rain forest. And we also found lots of strange-looking insects, and even an armadillo. But we couldn't find one monkey. After two and a half hours, we sat on a log and broke out the trail mix.

"Do you think we're the control group or something?" Bess wondered.

"What do you mean?" I asked, chewing on some dried cranberries and cashews.

"Mary wouldn't give us the data before we left because she didn't want us to be biased," Bess explained. "Maybe there are no monkeys on this trail, and she didn't want to tell us until later."

"It could be," I said. "But I had the sense that there were monkeys in every part of the rain forest. That's what Dan made it sound like, anyway."

Bess grinned. "Maybe he was just trying to impress you."

I tilted my head in thought. "Why would he do that?"

"Never mind," said Bess, exchanging a wry smile with George.

George swallowed a gulp of water and wiped her mouth with the back of her hand. "Maybe monkeys like to sleep late."

I tried to remember if I'd read anything about monkey sleep habits during my research. "I'm not sure—but we'll probably see some on the next hike."

Before we knew it, George's alarm beeped once to signal it was time to start over again.

As we followed the trail for a second time, George commented, "You know what's funny? We're here studying tourism's effect on wildlife, but the only tourists at the lodge are the researchers."

Bess nodded. "I know! I thought this resort was supposed to be so popular. Remember when we told Harold Safer we were going?"

Harold Safer is a friend from back home, who owns a local cheese store. He'd closed up his shop for a week to go on the research trip a few years ago, and was the person who suggested that the three of us sign up.

"He was so excited that we were going," I recalled. "Remember how he talked to us for twenty minutes about how beautiful the sunsets were from the lounge?"

"How could I forget?" asked Bess. "I kept trying to politely change the subject, but it didn't work." Harold likes to talk—a lot.

"He met people from all over the world," George remembered. "I think he still has pen pals in France and Brazil from that trip."

Just then I heard a rustling noise from overhead, so I motioned for my friends to stop.

"What is it?" Bess asked in a low voice as she peered up.

"To the left," I whispered, pointing at some branches.

We all stared, openmouthed, at the large group of monkeys in the tree.

"I think they're howlers," I said.

"But they're so quiet." Still George pulled out her computer and recorded the information. "Do you both see six?" she asked.

"Yup," I replied.

Bess nodded as she copied the information down into her notebook.

As George snapped her laptop closed, it locked with a small noise. Suddenly one of the howlers grunted. The others peered down at us and started bellowing. The noise seemed much worse than last night since the monkeys were so close.

"We should go," said Bess, backing up. "We don't want to scare them."

We ran off farther along the trail, not stopping until their howls were muffled and as quiet as elevator music.

George leaned over and placed her hands on her knees to catch her breath.

"You know what?" I asked. "We booked on out of there so we wouldn't scare the monkeys—but I think we're the ones who are scared!"

Bess and George grinned at me.

During our third hike of the day we found two other groups of monkeys—both of them of the refreshingly near-silent spider variety.

As we headed back to the lodge I said, "I thought

we'd see more capuchins, since they're supposed to be the most sociable."

"That's a good point," George agreed. "I wonder where they're hiding."

Pausing to tie my shoe, I noticed something on the ground. It was a wrapper from a candy bar. "I can't believe someone would be so careless—littering in a place like this!" As I picked it up I noticed something even stranger. "Bess, George? Come look at this."

We all examined the track marks carved into the mud. Bess, the resident mechanic, ran her fingers along the ground. "They're from an all-terrain vehicle," she stated.

"Are you sure?" asked George.

Bess nodded. "Positive. First of all, no other vehicle could make it through these narrow trails, but you can also tell by the width of the tires."

"That's really strange," I said. "As far as I know, there's no ATV at the resort."

"Then who could these belong to?" asked George.

"I have no idea," Bess answered, frowning at the ground. "It makes no sense whatsoever. We're deep in the rain forest, miles away from any other human beings."

I looked over my shoulder and shivered. "Well," I said, "we're *supposed* to be."

4

Trouble Ahead

As we headed back to Corcovado Ecologica I heard shouting in the distance. "I wonder what that's about," I said to my friends.

"It sounds like it's coming from the lodge," Bess replied as we quickened our pace.

When we reached the trailhead, I spotted two men. Though they weren't close enough to recognize, I could tell from the way they were waving their arms around that they were in the middle of a heated argument.

Bess, George, and I glanced at one another with raised eyebrows. Without a word we hurried down the hill.

Once we got closer, I realized who the men were: Jason and Bud.

Bud's face was so red it almost matched his cap. "If there are only three people working here, how can I not assume it was one of you?" he screamed.

"There are plenty of volunteers from River Heights!" Jason yelled back. His voice seemed different today—deeper and scratchier. "Did you ever suspect one of them?"

We stood merely a few feet away, but the men were too wrapped up in their argument to notice they had an audience.

I bit my bottom lip, hoping things didn't intensify between them.

"Everyone was busy with the research all day," Bud cried. "My group was the first one back."

Parminder must have heard the commotion too, because a minute after we arrived, she came hurrying over. "What's going on here?" she asked, looking back and forth between the two angry men.

"He stole my wide-angle lens," Bud said, pointing his finger at Jason.

Jason yanked a tissue from his pocket and blew his nose before answering. "Yeah, right."

Parminder put her hand on Bud's shoulder. "This is quite an accusation, Bud. Are you sure it was stolen? When did you see it last?"

Huffing out an angry breath, Bud explained, "It was sitting on top of my sleeping bag, in my tent, when we left this morning. I came back to find the tent flap partially open and the lens missing. I questioned Manuela and Lupa, but they said they were miles away, grocery shopping in town all day. Jason was the only person around here."

"Oh, dear," said Parminder.

Jason rolled his eyes. "Do you actually expect me to believe you? I've seen this scam a hundred times before. I'll bet you didn't even bring your wide-angle lens to Costa Rica. You just want to report it stolen so you can collect the insurance money, right?"

"I saw Bud's wide-angle lens yesterday in the taxi," George chimed in. "It's very fancy—of the highest professional quality."

Bud nodded furiously. "That's exactly what I told him!"

"So maybe you left it in the taxi," said Jason. "Did you ever think of that?"

"There's no way," Bud replied. "I've been on five continents in the past three years with all of my equipment and I've never lost a thing. Until today, that is."

"I'll say this one last time," Jason grumbled, getting right up in Bud's face. "I did not take your stupid camera lens! *Aah-choo!*"

"Bless you," I said.

Jason turned to me and blinked. "Thanks."

"Are you getting a cold?" I asked, trying to divert his focus away from his anger.

It didn't work. Shrugging, he said, "Who knows?" Then he took off toward the kitchen.

Bud took a deep breath before turning to the rest of us. "Please accept my apologies. This is so embarrassing. I rarely lose my temper, but this wide-angle lens was my favorite. I know exactly where I left it, and it couldn't have just disappeared. I asked Jason nicely at first, but he got so defensive so quickly. It made me incredibly suspicious. I don't know what came over me, but I just blew up."

"I can't believe this has happened." Parminder crossed her arms over her chest and shook her head. "I've been coming here for many years, and I assure you that we've never had this type of problem. I don't understand it."

Just then Mary joined us. "What's going on?" she asked.

"Nothing important," Parminder said. As Dan, Stephanie, and Benita wandered over, she changed the subject. "Well then, I'm very pleased to see that everyone made it back in time. We'll discuss our findings later on tonight."

I approached Bud after the group dispersed. "Maybe

I can help," I said. "Sometimes I'm able to find things that have gone missing."

"Yes, Dan told me about your talents," said Bud. "I would be very grateful for your help."

"Well, first we should go to the scene of the crime."

"Follow me," Bud said.

When he led me to his tent, I was surprised to see that Lupa was already there. She had a broom in her hand and was sweeping the path in front of the Reislings' tent. I'd planned on searching for footprints in the dust, but she'd destroyed the evidence. "Hi, Nancy. Hello, Bud. How are you doing?" asked Lupa.

Since there was no point in making her feel bad about her mistake, I said, "Not bad. What's new with you?"

"Not so much," Lupa replied. "I'm just trying to get this place cleaned up. Any luck with your lens?"

"Not yet," said Bud.

"That's a shame," Lupa replied. "I wish I hadn't been away all day. Maybe we could have prevented this."

"It's not your fault," said Bud. "I shouldn't have left the lens out in the open like that. Although I didn't think anyone would go inside my tent. I'd heard this place is very safe."

"It's very surprising," Lupa said thoughtfully.

"We've never had a problem with theft before."
Slinging the broom over her shoulder, she walked
away.

"Everyone keeps telling me that," Bud commented glumly. "But unfortunately, it doesn't exactly
help my situation."

I followed Bud into his tent and searched for other
clues, asking him all about the lens and where he last
saw it. There wasn't much to go on just then, but I assured Bud that I would keep thinking.

When I got back to our tent, Bess and George
asked me how everything went. "Well, I couldn't find
the lens, and I'm going to have a hard time finding
out who took it," I said. I explained that Lupa had
swept away all traces of footprints.

George shook her head. "I can't believe Jason is
stealing from his guests. No wonder the lodge is so
empty! Who'd want to stay here when you have to
worry about burglaries?"

"Whoa, slow down. We don't know for sure that
the lens was stolen," I reminded her.

"You're right," George said. "It's just that his wide-angle lens was so nice. I'd never seen a model like it
before. By the way, only a professional photographer
would have one. In fact, it wouldn't even fit on a normal type of camera."

I puzzled over this for a few moments, trying to

make sense of it all. "We're in the middle of the rain forest. Why would anyone steal a lens that could only be used with a professional's camera?"

"There's no way for a thief to know that," Bess pointed out.

"Too true," George said. "But we should warn Bud to keep an eye on his camera for the rest of the week. Once the thief—if it was stolen—discovers that he can't use the lens, he might go after the camera."

Before we could speculate further, the dinner bell rang. We hurried to the dining area.

Lupa set down a large plate of ham. "I didn't get a chance to ask you before," she said. "What did you think of the rain forest?"

"It was amazing," I answered. "And I love how all the thick trees provide natural air-conditioning."

"We sure need it," said Lupa. "This is one of the hottest dry seasons we've had in years."

That was one more thing I had to get used to. Instead of four seasons like back home, Costa Rica has only two—rainy and dry.

"We also saw the cutest little frogs," I continued.

"The orange ones with the blue legs?" asked Manuela, coming up behind her mother.

I nodded. "Yes. How did you know?"

"They're very common here. They're called poison-arrow frogs because they have special chemicals in their skin that will cause paralysis, or even death, if eaten by certain types of animals."

"You're kidding!" I exclaimed as I tried to remember if I had touched any of the frogs.

Manuela must have read my mind. "Don't worry," she said. "Their toxins are so weak, humans can handle them without a problem." Holding up a large glass pitcher, she asked, "Would you like some water?"

"Sure," I said. "Thank you."

As she poured me a glass I noticed that Cathy, who was sitting next to me, looked very glum.

"I guess you know about the lens," I said.

Cathy sighed. "Yes, I gave it to Bud for our anniversary last year. I can't believe someone stole it out of our tent. Bud told me you were going to find the thief, though. I can't wait to give him or her a piece of my mind!"

Suddenly Manuela gasped and dropped the pitcher of water. It hit the bench, first splashing water everywhere, and then shattered on the ground.

"I got you all wet, Nancy," Manuela cried. "I'm so sorry!" She swiftly handed me some napkins and then bent down to clean up the mess.

I slid off my bench so I could help her. "It's only water."

"I'm so clumsy," she said, placing the largest pieces of glass in her apron.

"It's not a big deal at all," I assured her, wondering why she was so nervous.

"That's easy for you to say," said Manuela.

"Are you okay?" I whispered. "What was it that surprised you?"

Manuela didn't answer me. "I need to get back to the kitchen," she said instead, hurrying off.

Lupa began to clean up the rest of the glass. "Manuela ran off in such a hurry," I said. "Is something wrong?"

"No, no. Everything's fine." Lupa flashed me a stiff, seemingly forced smile. "Please don't worry about it."

But not only was I worried—I was totally confused. Why would Manuela react so strangely when we were talking about the thief? Did she know something?

Later that night we gathered in the lounge to discuss our findings. "Let's start with Nancy's group," Parminder said.

Bess answered for us, handing the head scientist her notebook. "Nancy, George, and I saw three groups of monkeys: one troop of very noisy howlers on our second hike, and two groups of spider monkeys on our third hike."

Parminder turned to her with a puzzled expression. "You girls took the Ocean View Trail, correct?"

"Yes." I nodded.

"And you stuck to it?"

George said, "Absolutely. I kept track of our entire day, if you'd like to double-check."

"No, I trust you." Parminder frowned down at Bess's notebook. "It's just, well, never mind. How did everyone else do?"

Mary sighed and said, "We found only four groups of monkeys."

"My group saw just five," said Dan. "Not nearly as many as last year."

"Yes," said Parminder. "The Reislings and I had similar results, but I was hoping that we were the only ones."

George and Bess looked at me with raised eyebrows. All I could do was shrug back.

"This is all so odd," said Parminder, holding up a manila folder. "I have last year's results right here." She opened it up and started to read. "The girls on the Ocean View Trail should have seen at least nine groups of monkeys. And the other groups should have spotted even more than that."

"I don't understand what happened," said Mary, tucking a strand of hair behind her ear. "It's not like we can blame the tourists—there aren't any here."

"What do you think is keeping the monkeys away?" I asked Parminder.

The head scientist shrugged her shoulders. "I wish I knew. This type of thing has never happened before. Esteban would know the answer, I'm sure. But who knows what happened to *him*?"

Just then something occurred to me. "Could this have anything to do with the ATV tracks we found on the Ocean View Trail?" I asked.

"What are you talking about?" Mary exclaimed. "ATVs aren't even allowed in the state park."

5

Suspicion Grows

As soon as the alarm went off the next morning, I noticed that Bess was already up and dressed in a pair of light blue shorts and a matching T-shirt. Digging through her backpack, she said, "Now where did I put the socks that go with this outfit?"

Yawning and stretching, George crawled out of her sleeping bag. "I slept so well," she said.

"Me too!" Bess agreed. "It was so nice and quiet."

I was about to agree with them, but before the words came out, a thought occurred to me. "Wait a minute," I said. "Something's happened to the howler monkeys!"

George slipped on her hiking boots and frowned. "It's only our second night here. We don't know if they howl every single night," she reasoned. "Maybe they didn't run into any predators last night, and that's why they were quiet."

"Maybe," I said with a frown, wondering if I was overreacting. I had a strange feeling about it, but I decided to wait and see how the day went before jumping to any conclusions. After getting dressed and washing up I headed over to the dining area.

"Nancy, is this some new style no one told me about?" Dan asked, pointing to my shirt.

"Huh?" I glanced down at myself, completely mystified. Suddenly realizing what he was talking about, I slapped my palm to my forehead. I was so preoccupied earlier that I hadn't realized I'd put my T-shirt on inside out *and* backward. Oops.

"Where have you been?" I said, thinking quickly. "I thought everyone knew all about this new rain forest trend!"

Dan laughed. "Why am I always the last to hear about these things?"

From across the table George shook her head and tried to suppress a smile. She was used to me putting shirts on backward—and worse. Whenever I'm focused on a mystery, I tend to lose my focus on details like clothes. I'm just glad Bess wasn't there to see it, because she always gets much more distressed by these fashion faux pas of mine than George or me. Hurrying so as not to catch Bess, I excused myself to go to the bathroom and returned with my shirt on right.

As Lupa placed a large bowl of oatmeal on the table my focus shifted. "I don't understand how such a stunning place could be so empty," I thought out loud. It was my attempt to fish for some information.

Lupa took the bait. "I guess it's just not that popular anymore," she said with a shrug. "Who knows how or why?"

"Where's Manuela?" I wondered aloud.

"She slept late," Lupa answered quickly. "I'm sure she'll be here momentarily."

Dan brushed his hair out of his eyes. "When my brother, Jim, came to Costa Rica last month, he tried to book a tent here but couldn't."

"Why not?" I asked.

"According to its Web site, this place was booked solid," Dan replied.

"That's so strange," Lupa said as she set a pitcher of milk in the center of the table. "This place hasn't been completely booked in many months."

"I was talking to Jason last night about his computer system," George said. "He told me that most of the reservations at Corcovado Ecologica are secured online. Maybe that's where the problem lies."

"You mean it could be some sort of computer glitch?" asked Dan.

George shrugged. "I know it sounds too easy, but you never know. It's entirely possible." Turning to me, she said, "Nancy, you should e-mail Ned and ask him to try and make a reservation for the lodge. It'd be interesting to see what happens."

Dan looked back and forth between me and George. "Who's Ned?" he asked.

"My boyfriend," I told him.

"Oh."

I was suddenly relieved that George said something about Ned in front of Dan, because I had no time to deal with any romantic complications. I had a case to crack.

Just then Bess joined us, beaming. She was carrying a colorful Hawaiian print sarong, and she held it up to show the group. "Isn't this the greatest?" she asked.

"Now *that's* what I call a real rain forest trend," said Dan, winking at me.

"Well, thank you," Bess replied, obviously missing our joke.

"That sarong is so utterly fabulous!" Stephanie squealed as she and her sorority sisters joined us.

"Where's it from?" asked Kara.

"The gift shop." Bess wrapped the sarong around her waist. "Don't you love how it's so tropical? It totally fits in with the atmosphere. And with the rate of exchange for U.S. dollars to Costa Rican colóns, it was a total bargain!"

"Are there any more?" asked Elise. "That would be the perfect souvenir for my little sister."

"There are a bunch," Bess replied. "And with the resort so empty, I'm sure they won't be selling out anytime soon."

As they continued their conversation I managed to sneak off. I found Jason locking up his office.

"Hey there, how are you doing?" I called.

"Oh, hello, Nancy," Jason replied.

Ignoring his impatient tone, I asked, "Can I please borrow the resort's computer for a few minutes?"

Jason sighed. "I suppose I should be glad you don't want to charge your laptop battery like your friend George did. Do you know how high the electricity bills get out here?"

I put on my kindest grin, even though inside I was wondering why he was making such a big deal out of my small request. "Don't worry," I said. "I didn't even bring my computer. It's just that I promised my dad I'd e-mail him when I arrived, and I forgot to last night. He gets really worried when I'm away from home."

Since Jason just frowned, I kept talking. "To be completely honest, I'm feeling a little homesick." I blinked at Jason innocently, hoping he'd fall for my little bluff.

Jason seemed annoyed, but he opened up his office and pointed to the computer. "Try to make it quick, please."

"Will do," I said. "And thanks a bunch."

"Make sure you close the door when you go. It'll lock automatically."

After Jason left me alone, I didn't get right to my e-mail. Not when one of my prime suspects left me alone in his office! I had to snoop around a little.

I soon discovered that Jason was as disorganized as he was rude. The room was covered with stacks of papers, half of which had fallen from his desk and spilled onto the floor. I found receipts from bills paid, correspondence with guests, and letters to the resort owner in San Jose. Just lots of boring documents, and nothing that would help me solve the case.

Turning to the computer, I quickly logged onto my e-mail and wrote to Ned.

Dear Ned,

Greetings from beautiful Costa Rica! The environmental research here has been interesting, to say the least. I've seen three species of monkeys so far—all cute, but some noisier than I'd like. I hope you've been having

fun in River Heights. I was wondering if you could do me a small favor. Can you please go to the Corcovado Ecologica Web site and try to make a reservation for arrival tomorrow night? And once you get a response, can you forward it to me? This is very important. I don't have time to explain why right now, but I promise I will when I get home. Can't wait to see you.

Yours truly,
Nancy

After I sent the message to Ned, I e-mailed my dad. I didn't tell him that I was in the midst of—well, a *few* new mysteries. Dad is proud of my detective work, and he was all for my coming to Costa Rica, but sometimes he worries that I'll end up in a dangerous situation. It could be because I'm all the family he has, since my mom died when I was three. That's why I worry about him sometimes. Back at home it's just the two of us, and our housekeeper, Hannah Gruen—which reminded me of something. I told my dad to send my love to Hannah, and to thank her for suggesting that I bring my rain gear. She was right—as always. Just as her late cousin's sister-in-law had warned her, the rain forest is very wet.

When I returned to the table, I saw that I'd missed

something: Mary was searching underneath the table. Kara and Benita were rifling through their backpacks, and Stephanie was talking to Lupa.

What's going on now? I wondered.

Stephanie threw her hands up in the air and cried, "My binoculars have disappeared!"

"I'll bet they ended up in the same place as my wide-angle lens," said Bud, nodding toward Jason's office.

Parminder quickly joined us. She looked very distressed. "Now let's not jump to any conclusions."

"When did you last see them?" I asked, quickly surveying the area.

"Just twenty minutes ago," said Stephanie. "I got here early this morning, before anyone else, and I set them down on the bench before I went to use the bathroom. I didn't even realize that they were gone until just now." Suddenly she looked up at Lupa. "Where's Manuela? Maybe she knows something."

"Why would Manuela know anything?" I asked.

"She was the only other person here first thing this morning," said Stephanie.

Lupa hurried into the kitchen, calling over her shoulder, "I'll check with her later."

It was so strange! Lupa told me Manuela had slept late. An innocent mistake? Or was she hiding something?

I started following her, but Mary called, "Nancy, where are you going? It's just eight thirty and we really need to head out. Stephanie, I'm sure your binoculars will turn up later."

Stephanie frowned, mumbling, "Right."

After running to the tent to grab my canteen, I met Bess and George at the trailhead.

"Look at that," said Bess, pointing up into a tree. We were halfway through our third hike of the day and had spotted only one group of monkeys.

I followed her glance, then scanned the branches. "I don't see anything."

"To the left," said Bess. "That thing that looks like a football."

"What is it?" George wondered.

The animal was about two feet long. Hanging upside down in the tree and with brown fur that almost matched the bark, it was barely recognizable. It hardly moved, but I could see a slight rise and fall in its chest as it took slow, shallow breaths. "It's a sloth!" I exclaimed. "That's so cool."

"It doesn't even look alive," Bess marveled.

"They sleep for fifteen hours a day," I said, remembering my reading from the nature guide that Ned lent me before I'd come to Costa Rica. "Their camouflage is their main source of protection against predators. They don't even need to be awake to protect themselves!"

"I much prefer that to the howler monkeys' methods," said George as she snapped a few shots.

We moved on, searching high and low for monkeys, but finding only two troops of capuchins over the course of the entire day.

I glanced at my watch and frowned. "We still have over an hour left before sunset. Why don't we follow the ATV tracks to see where they lead?"

I led my friends through the brush, where we found the tracks lined with even more garbage.

"I hate it when people trash beautiful places like this." George picked up an old candy bar wrapper and placed it in her backpack.

"This is exactly what Parminder and the other scientists have been working so hard to avoid," I said.

Bess grimaced. "The litter is actually small potatoes next to the fumes those ATVs give off. They've been outlawed for a reason."

I bit my bottom lip. It was hard for me to believe that someone could be so careless about preserving the natural beauty of such a spectacular place.

After another half a mile, George and I added an ant-filled pretzel bag and two soda cans to our collection of garbage.

Bess went on ahead. She suddenly stopped at the base of a large tree and cried, "Oh, my!"

"Did you find a clue?" asked George.

"Nope," said Bess. "This is much better." She picked up a colorful feather, and held it up to the fading light. "Won't this look amazing with my new sarong? It's got to be the most perfect accessory!"

I looked at the feather. With its bold red, yellow, green, and blue stripes, it *was* really beautiful. There were many more scattered around the base of the tree. I wondered where they came from. I looked around and then up toward the sky, hoping to catch a glimpse of a tropical bird. Instead I noticed something strange caught up in one of the highest branches. Was that what I thought it was?

Crash Landings

"Hey," I said, nodding up to the tree. "Check it out."

George looked up from her GPS. "What is it?"

"Over to the left." I pointed at the strange thing I'd spotted in the top branches of the tree. It looked like some sort of net, but there was only one way to find out for sure. I had to get closer.

Of course, this was easier said than done. The net was so high up I could barely see it, let alone reach it. The tree was massive—much too large to grip. At one point the trunk split into a Y. I knew I'd be able to shimmy up the space between the branches fairly easily. The problem was getting up there. The trunk didn't split until very high up—way over my head, and far out of reach.

"Can someone give me a boost?" I asked.

After Bess finished gathering the feathers, she clasped her hands together, creating a step. "Here you go."

Hoisting myself up and using George's shoulder to steady myself, I struggled to grip the smooth bark, desperately reaching for the bottom of the Y split. But it was still way too high.

"Are you almost there?" asked Bess.

"Nope." I gasped, straining to stay upright. "Not even close."

As she tried to raise me higher her hands wobbled slightly, and I started losing my balance. Suddenly I felt myself tipping over. I grabbed for the tree, but there was nothing to hold on to. My hands slid along the bark, and a split second later I was falling straight down!

I tumbled over, taking Bess with me with an "Ooof!" I managed to land hands first in a pile of soft mud—but it still hurt.

George, who'd managed to jump out of the way, helped both of us get up. "You guys okay?" she asked.

"Fine." Bess straightened out her headband. Then she unraveled the bandanna she'd tied to her belt loop and began to wipe furiously at a small spot of mud on her shorts.

When she noticed me, her eyes got wide and she

handed me the bandanna. "Nancy, you need this more than I do."

Looking down, I realized I was covered in mud from head to toe. "Uh, I don't think that'll quite do the trick—but thanks!" Brushing my hands along my pants, I stared up into the tree. "But I still have to get that net."

Bess secured her hands once more, giving me another boost. I focused harder on the space where the trunk split, willing myself closer. Taking a deep breath, I lunged for it.

This time I was successful. Holding on tightly, I pulled the rest of my body up and managed to swing one leg through the space between the branches.

After pausing to catch my breath, I shimmied straight up.

"So is that what we think it is?" George called.

Stretching my arm as far as I could, I reached for the net. On the third try I managed to pry it loose, but when I tossed it to George and Bess, I made my first mistake. I meant to look down just for a second to make sure the net didn't catch on a lower part of the tree, but once I looked I couldn't turn away. The ground seemed so far away. I was transfixed, and a little dizzy.

Suddenly the branch swayed. I imagined it snapping in two—and myself plunging down headfirst. Before I knew it, I was overcome by a wave of nausea.

"You okay up there?" George looked concerned.

"Don't look down," Bess advised. But her warning came a little too late.

I wrapped my arms around the branch and closed my eyes for a few moments, taking deep, steady breaths. No time to panic. Everything would be all right.

When I opened my eyes, I focused on the sky. Through the leaves I could see that the sun was setting, creating beautiful swaths of orange and pink. Of course, this also meant that it would be dark before we knew it. We needed to get back to camp—fast.

I made my way carefully down the tree, keeping my eyes up. At the base of the split, I crawled to one side. Before I swung my feet down, I glanced at the ground to make sure that it was clear. Next, I dropped my legs, holding on to the tree with just my hands. Finally, I closed my eyes and let go.

I landed with a splat in the same puddle of mud, but this time I was able to steady myself before falling.

Getting up, I hurried over to my friends, who were examining the net a few feet away.

"There's something caught in it," said Bess.

When I got closer, I noticed a small patch of soft,

brown fur tangled in the knots. It looked as if it belonged to a monkey.

"We'd better head to the lodge," said George, gazing up at the sky and then at her watch. "Sunset is in eleven minutes."

I folded the net and carefully placed it in my backpack. Then we followed the ATV tracks back to the trail, making it to the lodge just after dark.

We found the three scientists huddled over some papers in one corner of the dining area when we got back.

"Hi," I called as we walked in. "How did everything go today?"

Dan looked up. "Not so well, I'm afraid. We found even fewer monkeys than yesterday."

"Yeah, same here," said Bess.

"At this rate, by tomorrow we'll be in the negative numbers," Mary added. "Or we would be, if that were possible."

"Are you just getting back from your hike now?" asked Parminder, scanning my mud-slathered clothes.

"Yes," I said. "We finished a little early so we decided to follow those ATV tracks I told you about. We didn't get to take them all the way because we ran out of time. But we did find something you'd be interested in." I handed Parminder the net.

"You found this in a tree?" she asked.

"Yup," George said. "Nancy did. It was pretty high up, too."

As the scientists examined it, Mary was the first to speak. "It's fur from a howler monkey," she stated. "It looks like someone's capturing them, but I don't understand why."

Dan cleared his throat. "It doesn't make any sense. The monkeys aren't particularly valuable—they're not even endangered."

We all stared at one another, perplexed.

Bess coughed and said, "This is a horrible thought, but perhaps someone is using them for some other purpose? Like for their fur?"

Mary frowned. "I suppose anything is possible, but I've never heard of such a thing."

Dan agreed. "Monkey fur is very rough, so it's not good for coats. And apparently their meat tastes horrible."

As the dinner bell rang, Stephanie and Benita walked by. "We just picked out some sarongs," they called to Bess, holding up two packages.

"Great!" said Bess, waving.

Parminder lowered her voice. "Do you mind if I keep the net for a little while?"

"No," I said. "Go ahead."

"Thanks," she replied. "And can we keep this between us for now? I don't want the others to worry."

"No problem," said George.

The three of us hurried to our tent so we could wash up before eating.

As Bess changed into her new sarong I said, "This is getting so complicated."

George sank down onto her bed. "Do you think everything is related? I mean the empty lodge and Esteban's disappearance and the missing monkeys?"

"Don't forget about the petty thefts," said Bess. She pulled her hair up into a bun and put one of the colorful feathers behind her ear. "Okay, I'm ready."

"Me too." I swiftly headed for the door.

"Nancy, wait," Bess called.

I turned around, asking, "What?"

She held a mirror up to my face. My hair was a tangled mess. Bess never let messy hair get by. I ran a hand through it to make her happy, and threw on one of George's baseball caps. "Better?"

"It'll do," Bess replied.

"Gee, thanks!" I said, a little sarcastically. Much as I loved Bess, I wished she'd let one bad outfit or bad hair day get by. Especially since they seemed to happen to me so often.

Once we made it back to the dining area, Mary noticed the feather in Bess's hair right away. "That's a beautiful scarlet macaw feather," she said.

"Is that what it is?" asked Bess. "I was going to

look it up in my field guide after dinner."

Mary dished some rice and beef stew onto her plate as she explained. "Scarlet macaws are extremely rare and endangered. You're lucky to have spotted some."

"Oh, I didn't," Bess said. "I found these feathers on the ground."

Out of the corner of my eye, I noticed that Jason was just leaving his office. I excused myself from the table and hurried over to him. "Jason!"

"Yes, Nancy?" he asked tiredly.

"Think I could use your computer for a few minutes? I need to check my e-mail again."

He sighed. "Don't you want to eat dinner?"

I couldn't even think about food at the moment. There were too many other things on my mind. For one, I wanted to see if Ned had replied, but of course I didn't say so. "I won't be long," I told him. "Promise."

Jason let me into the office. It only took me a second to realize that nothing had changed—the place was just as messy as it had been the last time I'd seen it.

Turning to the computer, I signed on to my e-mail and found two new messages—one from Ned and one from Dad. Dad wrote a quick hello, saying he was glad I was having a good time, and that I wasn't missing anything in River Heights. Next I opened up Ned's message.

Dear Nancy,

It's great to hear from you. I'm so glad you're all having fun in Costa Rica. Have you stumbled across a new mystery yet? I tried to make a reservation at Corcovado Ecologica, but could not. I got a message back almost immediately, and it said that the lodge was completely booked through the end of the year. I hope this helps.

River Heights isn't the same without you. I miss you and I can't wait to see you next week. Have fun and be careful!

Yours truly,
Ned

I grinned and fired off a quick note back, thanking Ned for his help, and writing that I missed him, too.

Then I went to find Jason, because we had some business to discuss.

While it was true that Jason had been very rude ever since we'd gotten to the lodge, that didn't make him guilty of anything other than being rude. And I hadn't found anything suspicious in his office. I couldn't imagine that he knew his computer system was faulty. Maybe his bad attitude was all about stress over the fact that the resort was so empty.

In my heart of hearts, I hoped he'd be happy that I'd discovered the computer glitch. Maybe he'd be able to get it fixed right away. The resort would be busy again, and he'd be able to afford to rehire his staff. They would clean the place up, and all would return to normal. Even though this didn't explain Esteban's disappearance, the petty theft, or even the missing monkeys, it was something—and I was pretty excited to give him the good news.

Before I found Jason, though, I ran into George, who was on her way back to the dining hall from the bathroom. I quickly filled her in on my discovery.

George didn't seem surprised at all. "Something similar happened once on my mom's catering business Web site," she explained. "We meant to send an automatic message saying we'd be away for the week—this was last summer when my family rented the cabin up at Lake Firefly—but instead the message said 'We're closed'—as if it was indefinite. We lost a ton of business."

"That stinks," I said.

"It did." George nodded. "Anyway, my point is that I know how to fix the problem. If Jason wants, I'd be happy to reprogram the site."

I smiled at her, saying, "That sounds terrific. I can't wait to give Jason the good news!"

We found him a few minutes later, reading a magazine in the lounge.

"Jason?" I asked.

He looked up and frowned at me. "You locked my office behind you, right, Nancy?"

I nodded. "Yes, of course. I wanted to tell you something, though. I had reason to believe that the Corcovado Ecologica Web site was faulty, so I had a friend from River Heights do a little experiment."

Jason looked at me suspiciously. "What kind of experiment?" he asked slowly.

"Dan told me that his brother tried to make a reservation at the lodge last month, but he got a message back saying it was booked. It seemed strange, since you told me that this place has been empty for months. So I had my friend try booking a tent for tomorrow night, knowing there are plenty of free places. But he couldn't. Ned got a message saying that Corcovado Ecologica was filled to capacity."

George took over. "It's probably due to a simple computer problem. I've seen this type of thing before—I can fix it for you."

I'd expected Jason to be at least a *little* grateful. So I was shocked when he shouted, "I don't want either of you anywhere near my computer. And from now on, my entire office is off limits!"

"But it's just a simple problem," said George. "All I need is, like, twenty minutes. A half an hour, tops."

"Just mind your own business," Jason growled, throwing his magazine down on the ground and storming off.

We both stood there frozen, staring after him. "What was that about?" asked George.

"I've no idea," I had to admit. "But I think you were right to suspect him from the beginning."

"Suspect him of what?" asked George.

"Well—that's the problem." I bent down and picked up the magazine that Jason had been flipping through. It was called *Exotic Birding*. Tucking it under my arm, I turned to George and replied, "I'm not sure what he's guilty of, but it's something."

7

A Rain Forest Romance

As soon as George and I made it back to the dining area, Dan asked, "Is everything okay?"

"Fine." I bluffed, forcing a smile. "Everything is great."

"Must be trouble with the boyfriend," Dan guessed.

"Nope," I said. "Things with Ned are the same as usual—really great."

"Okay," Dan replied, frowning. "I was just asking, and if you want to talk about anything, I'm here."

Mm-hmm. Like I'd talk to Dan about trouble with Ned—*if* I had any!

Bess stared at me with pursed lips. I sensed she knew something was wrong, and that it had nothing to do with Ned. Of course, she also knew to save her questions for when we were alone. "You should eat something, Nancy." She pushed my plate toward me gently. "You must be starving."

After dinner I took a walk on the beach, trying to make sense of it all. The night was clear. The full moon reflected off the calm water, providing so much light I didn't even need the flashlight I was carrying. Of course, my mind was flooded with too many questions to enjoy the totally beautiful surroundings.

Why had Jason reacted so defensively when George and I were only trying to help? Was he keeping the lodge empty on purpose, so no one would find out he was kidnapping monkeys? If so, what did he want with them, when all three scientists assured me the monkeys weren't valuable in any way, shape, or form? Furthermore, did any of this have to do with Stephanie's missing binoculars or Bud's missing wide-angle lens? And what about Esteban? There were too many missing pieces to this puzzle—and time was running out. We had to fly back to River Heights in just five days.

When I headed back to my tent, I heard a strange noise. The sound was muffled, and it was coming from a group of palm trees.

I crept over and found Parminder sitting in a hammock. Her face was buried in her hands and she was crying.

"Are you okay?" I asked as I approached.

Startled, she looked up at me. "Oh hello, Nancy."

I handed her a tissue and asked, "What's wrong?"

She blew her nose. "It's nothing."

"People don't cry over nothing," I said, sitting down in the next hammock. "But if you don't want to talk about it, I understand."

Even though Parminder smiled at me weakly, there was so much sadness in her dark eyes. "I'm afraid there's not much to talk about."

"Is the disrepair of the lodge disturbing you this much?" I asked. "Or are you more upset about the missing monkeys?"

"Well, the lack of monkeys is indeed a strange turn of events after what had been many years of successful research," Parminder replied. "But to be completely honest, it's not just my work. I'm crying over Esteban, the resident biologist who used to work here. You see, I didn't tell you the whole story about him."

"What do you mean?" I asked.

"We're in love," Parminder cried. "Or at least, I am. It happened five years ago on a research trip just like this one."

My heart went out to Parminder. "Oh, no!"

"We've been together ever since," she continued. "But of course, we only see each other during summer and winter vacations."

"That must be so hard."

Parminder nodded sadly. "It *has* been, which is why I wanted Esteban to move back to River Heights with me this year. I even found him a research position at the university. But Esteban wasn't sure. I didn't blame him—he had his homeland to consider. I was giving him time to think about it, and he was supposed to make a decision by this week."

Shaking my head, I finished her story. "But instead, he disappeared."

Parminder wiped her tears away. "I didn't think that Esteban was the type of person to do this sort of thing. I wonder if his absence means he wants to stay in Costa Rica and he can't bear to tell me, or if it's something else altogether. I honestly don't know whether I should be angry with him for leaving, or scared because he's missing."

I thought about this for a few moments before answering her. "You know, if Esteban is as wonderful as you say he is, I can't imagine him disappearing with no word. There must be more to the story."

Parminder wiped the dampness from her eyes. "Do you think so?"

"Yes. I really do," I assured her.

Parminder smiled weakly. "I appreciate your thoughtfulness, Nancy. And it feels good to talk about this. But I'd better finish up my field notes before I get too sleepy." After waving good-bye, she stood up, shone her flashlight in front of her, and headed back to the lodge.

By the time I got back to the tent, I was even more determined to uncover the mystery—and I had a plan.

"Hey guys, are you ready to get to the bottom of this mess?" I asked as I charged through the tent's opening flaps.

"Are we ever," said Bess, looking up from the novel she was reading by flashlight. "Just the thought of those poor, missing monkeys makes my heart ache."

"I agree. Monkey-napping is just plain evil," said George. "So tell us, Nancy. What's the plan?"

Placing my hands on my hips, I grinned. "Well, with four search parties out in the rain forest all day, whoever is meddling with the monkeys is doing so after hours. Right?"

"But we're only in the rain forest between eight thirty and five o'clock," said Bess. "That still leaves so much time."

"Not necessarily," I replied. "Sunset is at six, and there are no lights in the rain forest. That means our suspect is working in the morning. So in order to investigate, we must be in the forest at sunrise."

"Do you think we'll catch whoever is responsible?" asked George.

"I can't say for sure," I admitted. "But we have to try."

8

Just Dropping In

Wake up, Nancy!" **George** shook my shoulder gently.

"Huh?" I asked. "Is something wrong?"

"The alarm on my watch must be broken," George said, "because it never went off. We were supposed to be up and out of here an hour ago!"

From the other side of the tent Bess yawned. "What did you say?"

George spun around. "We're late."

"Late for what? It's barely five A.M."

The words took a few moments to register, but once they did, I bolted up. Shoot! Our plan was to start hiking before sunrise. We only had a few minutes left. I leaped out of my sleeping bag and got dressed quickly, hoping we still had time to follow the ATV tracks and make it back by breakfast without anyone catching on to what we'd been doing.

Minutes later we crept to the trailhead. Not wanting to wake the scientists or any of the other volunteers, we didn't speak until we were far away from the tent area.

George, who was fiddling with the buttons on her watch, seemed very upset. "I don't know what happened."

"It's okay," I assured her. "We still might be able to see something, and if not, there's always tomorrow morning." I didn't let on how nervous I really was. Tomorrow was Wednesday and we were leaving first thing on Saturday. There was so much to figure out by then.

A yellow-and-green toucan squawked overhead. As I watched it soar over the treetops, I couldn't help but notice that the sky was quickly filling with gray storm clouds. They loomed overhead, like a sign that things were about to take a turn for the worse.

Bess followed my gaze and frowned. As soon as she slipped into her rain jacket, a bolt of lightning shot across the sky. Next a thunderclap boomed. It came from above, but seemed to pulse from all around us. Seconds later I felt a steady drizzle, which soon turned into a heavy storm. With our heads bent down, we trudged on through the forest.

Bess was well protected and George had a rain hat. I, on the other hand, left in such a hurry that I was completely unprepared for anything other than being soaked.

Wet clothes seemed like a trivial problem right now, though. The tracks were already starting to disappear into mud. We walked swiftly, yet gingerly, stepping over the tree roots that wound across our path, and occasionally slipping on the wet leaves. As the rain beat down harder and faster, it became difficult to see. I placed one hand over my eyes in an attempt to shade them from the rain, but it didn't do much good. The wind had picked up, and the drops nailed me from every direction.

Suddenly I tripped over a rock and grabbed on to Bess's arm to steady myself.

"You okay?" she asked.

"Fine." I bent down, slipped two fingers into my boot, and pulled out a large, sharp-edged pebble.

George and Bess went on ahead, stopping a few yards later.

"I think I see something," George said.

I hurried over. We'd stumbled across a small yet suspicious-looking clearing, and two men were standing in the center of it. They wore long, green ponchos, and wielded large, menacing-looking axes. They were felling a tree. Each time the ax made contact with the wood, a flat crack echoed through the forest.

Bess leaned in close and said quietly, "Do you think that one of those men is Jason?"

I pushed my sopping-wet bangs away from my eyes and squinted at the men. We weren't that far away, but the rain made it difficult to see. Add to that the big ponchos they were wearing, and there was no way I could make a positive ID. "I can't tell," I replied. "But I wouldn't be surprised."

An ATV and a group of empty cages sat at the edge of the clearing, but there was no sign of the monkeys. George carefully opened up her backpack and pulled out her digital camera. Aiming it at the men, she began taking pictures.

"Make sure you get plenty of shots of those cages," I said in a hushed voice.

"Do you think they're for the monkeys?" George asked as she snapped away.

"I don't know." As I stared at the scene before us, I bit my bottom lip. The cages were small and round at the top. Something about them seemed odd, but I couldn't put my finger on it. I searched the clearing for another clue, but the only one I came up with was the clearing itself. Obviously these men were up to no good. Not only were they driving outlawed ATVs, but the forest was part of a national park, which meant it was protected. People weren't allowed to just cut down trees wherever they felt like it.

Suddenly the men backed away from the tree. It swayed and then toppled, causing the ground to tremble. The men then dragged it away from us, through the thick of trees at the opposite end of the clearing, and left it there.

As one man started chopping away at another tree, his partner paced across the clearing. His lips moved, but as far as I could tell, he wasn't saying anything. He seemed to be counting. I guessed that he was measuring the clearing. They were obviously cutting down trees to widen the space, and surely they had a specific size in mind, but why were they doing this? *That* I couldn't figure out.

Bess and George grabbed my hands and squeezed. We all held our breath in anticipation, as the man paced merely a few feet from where we were crouched.

Since the bush only hid us from certain angles, if he took another few steps to the right, he'd definitely spot us. The storm stopped just as suddenly as it had begun. Everything became still and silent—until the man walked closer.

His footsteps splashed in the puddles. He flipped back the poncho's hood, so now, through the leaves, I could tell he was short and had long, dark hair pulled back into a low ponytail.

Just then the other man called something out in Spanish. The man closest to us turned around and walked the other way.

"That was close," Bess whispered.

"*Too* close," I replied. "We should get out of here." Turning to George, I asked, "Did you get enough pictures?"

"Almost." She pressed a button on the top of her camera and the zoom lens extended with a dull hum. George covered up the camera in an attempt to muffle the sound as we all kept our eyes on the men.

I breathed a sigh of relief when I realized they hadn't heard the noise.

A second later, though, something started beeping—loudly.

I glanced at George, panicked. "What's that?"

"I don't know," she said, fiddling with the camera. "Maybe it's low on batteries? This could be some sort of warning."

"They're going to hear us!" Bess warned, keeping a wary eye on the men.

Unable to stop the beeping, George finally shoved her camera into its case, and stuffed it inside her bag. Rather than becoming muffled, though, the beeping got louder. Yikes!

Just as I feared, one of the men turned around. He stared straight at the bush we were hiding behind, then he said something to the other man. Suddenly they both started heading toward us.

Knowing they'd reach us in a matter of seconds, my eyes darted around the forest.

As my friends and I trembled in our boots, I realized there was only one thing to do. "On the count of three, we're all going to run."

George and Bess looked at me wide-eyed.

"Okay, forget it," I said, swiftly amending my plan. "There's no time to count. Let's just run!"

We stood up and ran as fast as we could through the trees.

The men shouted and started chasing us. One of them continued to yell. I couldn't understand a word of what he was saying. But I didn't need to speak Spanish to understand that he was fuming.

I darted to the left, ducking under a low-hanging branch. "Be careful!" I called.

Luckily my friends cleared the branch with ease.

"Guess what?" George huffed a moment later. "The beeping was from my watch."

"That's technology for you," Bess muttered with sarcasm. "Always making your life so much easier!"

"How can you joke at a time like this?" asked George.

Suddenly an angry shout ripped through the forest. I stopped and spun around, fearing for my friends' safety. But it was one of the men who had fallen. He was writhing on the ground and moaning.

The other bent over him for just a moment. Noticing that we'd stopped too, he scowled and then continued chasing us.

In response, we picked up the pace.

As we got farther from the clearing, a sudden burst of confidence surged through me. Not only had we already gotten rid of one man—we were young, quick and nimble. Surely we could outrun the second!

Adrenaline pumping, I weaved in and out of the trees, turning left, and then right, and then left, again. Bess and George, both good runners, followed. Twigs and brush scraped at my calves, and mud splashed all over my legs, but the only thing I could focus on was getting my friends and myself to safety.

Minutes later, after regaining her breath, George said, "He's gone."

I glanced over my shoulder. The man was nowhere in sight. "Let's keep going," I said. "He probably can't see us either, but that doesn't mean he's not close."

We continued running for a little while longer. Only when I was absolutely positive that we'd shaken him did I slow to a quick walk. Breathing in deeply, we headed back toward a trail we'd crossed during the chase.

"Wow!" George huffed.

Bess shuddered. "That was a little too close for comfort."

"No kidding," said George. "I'm sorry about my watch. Talk about bad timing."

"And bad puns," Bess said, rolling her eyes and smiling.

"Hey, we're safe now." I grinned at my friends. "Don't worry at—*AAAHHH!*"

I couldn't finish my sentence because at that moment I felt the ground beneath me give way. I heard a loud crack and then suddenly went shooting straight down.

"Oof!"

Before I knew it, I'd landed on one foot. It rolled left as the rest of my body rolled right. Pain shot up from my ankle and seared through my entire body. My leg felt as if it was on fire, and tears sprang to my eyes.

Wiping them away, I looked around. I was deep underground in a dark space—some sort of trap! Blinking, I tried to take in my surroundings, but I couldn't see a thing.

Groping around, I found a soft, dirt wall. I leaned one hand against it, and I tried to stand up, but couldn't. The pain was too much.

Suddenly I heard something nearby—some rustling

and a series of grunting noises. I forgot all about the pain, because now I had bigger things to worry about. Scarier things.

Not only was I in some sort of trap, but I wasn't alone.

9

A Surprising Discovery

I was in a trap with someone else—but what could I do to get out of this? My ankle was throbbing, and I couldn't see two feet in front of my nose. My heart felt as if it was pounding in my throat, and I could actually feel the blood in my veins turning cold. Hearing shuffling nearby, I slowly turned my head toward the noise. I drew in my breath and called out into the darkness. "Hello? Who's there?"

No one answered me, but I could hear someone shifting about.

"I'm Nancy Drew. Who are you? Are you okay? How long have you been in here?"

Again my questions were met with silence. Shivers ran up and down my spine as I tried one last time, in an unsteady voice. "I'm here to help. Please answer me."

I heard some inaudible grunting—not exactly what I'd hoped to hear under the circumstances. I was even more upset to discover that whoever—or *whatever*—was in there with me was getting closer. I could feel breath on my face—and it wasn't too sweet. Willing myself to remain calm, I clenched my jaw and shuffled away. When my back hit the dirt wall, I was flooded with a horrible realization: I was cornered.

Whoever was with me seemed to smell my fear, because it continued to approach. When I felt a lot of warm breath on my cheek and something soft brush up against my neck, I screamed.

Whatever it was scurried away, with a shriek that didn't sound human.

Wait a minute . . . Could it be?

I groped at the ground, searching for something I could use to protect myself, but my fingers sifted through dirt, broken twigs, and small pebbles.

Suddenly a voice cried out from above. "Nancy, are you down there?"

It was Bess! Relief flooded through me as I looked up. "Help!" I yelled.

"George, come quick! She's down here!" Bess shone a flashlight down through the small hole at the top of the trap. Squinting at the light, I saw the outline of her head.

"We'll get you out of there—hold on," Bess said.

"Keep the flashlight on!" I cried. "And can you move it to the left a little?"

Bess did as I asked.

"Okay, great. Hold it right there." Taking a deep breath, I settled my gaze on eight pairs of eyes. Attached to those eyes were eight little capuchin monkeys, trembling in the corner and staring at me fearfully.

I clapped my hand over my mouth to stifle a laugh. "Did I frighten you?" I asked gently. "I'm so sorry!"

"Who are you talking to down there?" asked Bess.

"You'll see!" I called. One of the monkeys approached carefully. He sniffed at my shorts and brushed a furry paw against my leg.

Realizing that he was after my trail mix, I pulled the bag from my pocket. "Do you want this?" I dangled it in front of him. "Are you hungry?"

The monkey snatched the bag and his troop swarmed around him. They tore open the plastic and gobbled it down voraciously.

"How long have you been down here?" I asked. As my eyes adjusted to the light, I noticed that there were claw marks in the dirt sides—evidence that the monkeys had tried to crawl up and out, unsuccessfully. My heart went out to them, and at the same time, anger surged through me at the thought of someone treating innocent creatures this way. I was still puzzled as to why someone would go to such lengths to trap them, but two things were crystal clear. One, I would find whomever was responsible for this atrocity. And two, they would be stopped.

A few moments later a vine dropped down from above.

"It's secured up here," Bess explained. "We tied it to a thick tree. Just climb on up." She peered over the edge once more, moving her flashlight beam around. "Are those monkeys? How cute! Way to go, Nancy! You solved the mystery!"

"Yeah, thanks to my klutziness!" Grabbing the rope, I started to climb. I didn't make it very far. I've climbed out of holes, ditches, and caves before, so normally this type of thing wouldn't have been a problem, but this morning was a different story. My first step with my sprained ankle sent painful waves of shock through my entire body. I dropped the vine and tumbled down, landing with a thump.

"Nancy?" George called. "You okay?"

"I twisted my ankle," I yelled, "so I can't climb."

Bess peered down and I heard her confer with George. "Make yourself a harness, and we'll pull you up," she said a moment later. "Just tell us when."

I did as she asked, making two large loops in the vine and knotting them, rock-climbing style. After putting my legs through, I held on to the top of the vine with both hands and called, "Ready!"

My friends struggled to pull me up.

When the monkeys saw me rise, they started jumping about. "Don't worry," I called. "I won't leave you here."

Up I went. When I was near the top of the hole, Bess and George grabbed me under my arms and pulled me out.

"Whew!" Safely above ground, I collapsed in the dirt with my feet splayed out in front of me. "That was scary."

"What about the monkeys?" George asked. "Should one of us go down there to help them get up?"

I shook my head. "Not necessary. Just retie the vine around that large tree you told me about, and then drop the loose end back down into the trap. The monkeys will be able to figure things out from there."

Less than a minute after my friends followed my advice, the monkeys began their climb. Much more efficient than I, they were all out in less than a minute. They didn't hang around for long, either. Each one scrambled into the closest tall tree.

"Who would trap poor innocent monkeys like that?" Bess asked sadly.

"No one I want to come across," I said. "Hey, I bet

our friends with the axes are still lurking in the rain forest. We need to get back to camp. It's not safe out here." My friends happily agreed.

Before we left, we quickly fixed the trap, patching up the hole with fallen branches, twigs, and leaves. I was also sure to make note of my surroundings, homing in on certain landmarks—the boulder shaped like Texas and the extra-wide tree with the snakelike vines wrapped around its trunk. Should we end up here again, I wanted to be sure not to fall into the trap for a second time.

I draped one arm over each of my friends' shoulders and they helped me back to the lodge. We made it to camp just a few minutes after eight, to find that everyone was finishing up with breakfast.

"What happened to you three?" Dan asked.

I understood why he was a little suspicious. Not only was I limping—I was also soaked to the bone and covered from head to toe in mud. Even though George was walking normally, she didn't look much better. As for Bess, well, she managed to look all right. Somehow, she *always* manages to look all right.

"We decided to take a little hike before breakfast," I told the group. I wasn't being dishonest, but I still felt guilty, because what I told them was only a very small fraction of the truth.

As they eyed us with confusion, George added, "We got caught in the rain."

"You must have been out very early," said Parminder, staring at us with pursed lips.

I had every intention of telling the head scientist exactly what we saw. I just didn't want to do so in front of everyone else, especially with Jason around.

I gave Parminder a pleading look that said, "Please don't ask me about this right now."

She nodded slightly. She got it.

"Well, we'd better get changed," said Bess. "We don't want to be late for our hike."

It was hard to believe that our "regular" day hadn't even begun. I sank down onto the bench, too weary and in too much pain to walk another step.

"Want some help?" asked George.

I shook my head. "You guys go ahead. I just need to rest for a couple of minutes."

As my friends went to our tent, Dan moved over to where I sat. "What happened?"

"I tripped," I replied, pulling my leg up onto the bench and taking off my shoe and sock. As soon as I got a clear look at my ankle, I winced. It was bright red, and swollen to over twice its regular size.

Kara leaned over me and cringed. "Nancy, that doesn't look so good. I think you need some ice."

"I'll get it," said Dan.

As he hurried to the kitchen I realized I wouldn't be able to hike today. My ankle throbbed with pain, and I didn't want to slow down my friends. And then it struck me that if we ran into the ax-wielding men again, chances were that this time, I wouldn't be able to outrun them.

10

The Thief Strikes Again

Before everyone left, I took Parminder aside to fill her in on the latest. "I don't know what those men were up to," I finished, "but I can't say for sure that it's safe to go back into the rain forest."

Parminder frowned as she thought about this for a moment. "Those men were probably loggers. Esteban had to deal with them all the time. It's actually good news that there were only a couple. They're probably just trying to earn some extra cash by cutting down trees to sell, and on a small scale, they don't affect wildlife so drastically. It's not that I approve of this, but there's not much I can do. My work is about stopping large corporations from cutting down hundreds or even thousands of trees all at once."

"But they were chasing us with axes," I said. "I

couldn't understand what they were saying, but they were *really* mad."

"They were probably chasing you to keep you away from the area—not because they actually wanted to harm you. The fact that they were working so early in the morning means that they are trying to avoid us," Parminder reasoned. "This leads me to believe that our volunteers won't run into them, and if they do, that the men won't harm anyone."

"But what about the underground trap? There could be more. Are you sure it's safe for everyone to be out?"

"Trust me," Parminder replied. "I wouldn't send volunteers into the forest if I thought they were in any danger, which is why you must stay back today. Your ankle just shouldn't be walked on."

"You're sure you want to send everyone else out there?"

Parminder nodded stubbornly. "This trip has been disastrous in so many ways already. It's important that we continue with the research. I understand that you have your methods, but I would hate for anything to happen to you. Please be careful."

I promised her I would, then said good-bye to the rest of the group. Limping over to the tent, I changed out of my muddy clothes and took a shower. By now I was used to being in the wild, so I hardly jumped when I noticed the spider sharing the bathroom with me. Instead I focused on how wonderfully refreshing it felt to wash all of the dirt and grime off my body—how amazing it was to have fresh and clean running water out in the middle of nowhere.

Once I was back in the tent, I noticed that George had left her digital camera behind—my favorite of George's gadgets. I turned it on. I pulled up the shots on the tiny viewing window one by one, laughing at the early ones of my friends and me packing for our trip. In one, George wore a goofy smile as she pointed at Bess's seven hairclips—one for each day of our trip. The next pictured my dad, waving good-bye at the airport in River Heights.

Soon I got to the pictures from Costa Rica. I glanced at the ones taken on our first day—of the capuchin monkeys in the trees by the airport, and of Dan grinning with his arm around me. When I found the first picture of the cages in the clearing, I zoomed in on it. Something wasn't right. I sat up and focused.

It was then that I realized the cage doors seemed way too small for any monkey to fit through. And each cage seemed hardly larger than a capuchin. No way would anyone be able to squeeze a howler or spider monkey inside. This raised so many questions.

If the cages weren't for the monkeys, then what were they for?

I'd have to show the pictures to the scientists when they returned. Maybe they'd have a clue.

Suddenly I heard a strange rumbling noise. It was my stomach. I hadn't eaten since last night. Setting the camera down on George's bed, I limped over to the kitchen, where I found Manuela cutting mango for a fruit salad.

She looked up at me with surprise, asking, "You're not hiking today?"

"Unfortunately, no," I replied. "I sprained my ankle this morning."

"Oh, dear." Manuela glanced at me with sincere concern. "I hope you're okay."

"It's nothing serious," I assured her.

"I don't remember seeing you at breakfast." Manuela pulled some biscuits and jam from a cupboard and set them on a small table nearby. "You must be starving."

"Thanks so much." Easing myself down into the chair, I took a small bite of the biscuit. The moist crumbs almost melted in my mouth. "This is delicious!"

"Thanks." Manuela grinned. "I made them this morning. It's my mom's secret recipe."

"You're an excellent baker," I told her.

"I learned from the best."

I had some questions for Manuela—most of them nonbiscuit related. I decided to dive right in.

"How long have you and your mother been working here?"

"Well, my mother was first hired when I was a toddler, and this has been my home ever since. I hardly remember life before Corcovado Ecologica."

"You must really feel attached to this place," I said.

Manuela nodded. "It is wonderful."

"Can I help you with anything?"

"You can cut papaya," said Manuela, handing me an apron and a knife.

"I love papaya." As I tied the apron strings around my waist, I changed the subject. "Do you like working here?"

"It's all right," said Manuela. "I like helping out my mom, and it's all for a good cause. We're saving for my college tuition."

"College!" I said. "Why, you're so young."

"I know, but it's never too early to start planning. It's just three and a half years away, after all. I just hope that . . ." Rather than finish her thought, Manuela shook her head. Staring down at her feet she mumbled, "Never mind. I don't want to bore you with all of my troubles."

"Please tell me."

"Well," said Manuela. "Jason has fired so many people on the staff. I fear that my mother will be next. If it weren't for the River Heights group, we'd only be cooking for Jason and maybe his friends. We haven't had any real guests in so long, I don't know how he can afford to pay us."

Suddenly my ears pricked up. "Who are Jason's friends?" I asked. "I haven't seen anyone else around here."

"There were two men here," said Manuela. "But they didn't say much, so I'm not sure what their story is. Come to think of it, they left right before you arrived."

I had the sneaking suspicion that Jason's friends and the men with the axes were the same two people, but I didn't want to say anything until I was sure. "And you haven't seen them since?" I pressed.

Manuela frowned down at the fruit salad. "I'm positive, and I'd be afraid to ask Jason about it, anyway. He's been so short-tempered lately."

"Do you have any idea why? Have you ever asked?"

"Oh, no. I cannot talk to Jason," said Manuela. "Look what happened to Esteban."

This was a surprising statement. Once more, I felt a funny feeling in the pit of my stomach. "What do you mean? I was told that Esteban quit."

Worry lines appeared between Manuela's eyebrows as she set down her knife. "Esteban did no such thing. He asked too many questions and he got fired. But please, *please* don't tell Jason I told you."

"I would never," I promised. "I need to get to the bottom of this mystery, but I won't do it by betraying your trust."

Manuela smiled at me gratefully. "Dan told me you were a famous detective."

I felt my cheeks heat up at the thought of Dan talking about me. "I'm not famous. He exaggerates."

"Whatever you say," said Manuela. "Famous or not, I'm honored that you are trying to fix things here!"

I frowned down at the fruit salad. "Manuela, do you mind if I ask you about something else?"

"Anything," the young waitress replied. "I am happy to help."

"I've noticed that a lot of things have gone missing at the lodge. Do you have any idea why?"

Manuela paused for a moment, and then shrugged. "People lose things all the time. The empty lodge—Jason's behavior—*that's* the real problem here."

"But—"

Manuela raised one hand to cut me off. "I know nothing of the missing things, Nancy. And I must get going."

"But Manuela—"

It was too late to ask her any more questions. Manuela had raced out the back door, leaving me all alone.

I went to my tent to try and sort things out, but I drifted off to sleep before I could think about anything. When I woke up, Bess and George were back.

"How did everything go today?" I asked.

"We're so sorry to wake you, Nancy," Bess said. "We didn't mean to!"

I sat up and rubbed my eyes. "It's okay. If I don't get up now, I'll never sleep tonight."

"How's your ankle?" George asked.

"It's a little better," I said, glancing down. "It only hurts when I put pressure on it."

Bess said, "You should ice it again."

"Yes, I'll do that soon. But tell me, how was the hike?"

My friends shared a worried glance. Then George said, "I'm afraid we didn't see any monkeys."

Wow. "Not one?" I asked.

"There must be more underground traps like the one that you fell into," Bess reasoned. "Did you find anything out while we were gone?"

I nodded. "A lot, actually. First of all, Esteban didn't quit. He was fired. And second, Jason had two friends staying here, but they disappeared as soon as we arrived."

George's eyebrows shot up. "Do you think they might be the same men who chased us?"

"I think so," I replied. "But let's keep this to ourselves until we're sure. Oh—and how can I forget the most important news? I was looking at the pictures on the digital camera this morning, and I realized the cages we saw couldn't be for monkeys because monkeys wouldn't even fit inside. The doors are too small."

"Then what are they for?" asked Bess.

"That I don't know," I admitted. "But maybe one of the research scientists will. We should bring the camera with us to dinner."

"That sounds great," said George, rifling through her bag. "There's just one problem. I can't find it."

"I left it right there on your bed."

"It's not here now," she said.

Before I could think of what to say next, we heard shouting from outside our tent.

"I don't believe it!" someone bellowed.

"What now?" I wondered as we hurried outside.

Bud was holding Manuela by the arm, and he was angrier than ever. Poor Manuela was crying and struggling to break free.

"Let go of her, Bud! What's going on here?" I asked.

"I found our little thief!" Bud said snidely. "She was walking by my tent and she had my wide-angle lens hidden in her apron."

"I am not a thief," Manuela cried. "I was returning your wide-angle lens!"

"Because you realized you couldn't use it?" asked Bud angrily.

Manuela shook her head. "I would do nothing of the sort. I've never stolen anything. Honest!"

"Hold on a second," I said. "Everyone calm down. Bud, let Manuela explain herself. And while you're at it—let her go."

He dropped her arm reluctantly.

Manuela sniffed and wiped her tears away before speaking. "I was working in the kitchen as usual, and I happened to see something shiny out near the trash. I got closer and found the lens. I knew that Bud had lost it because I overheard his argument with Jason the other day, so I was returning it."

It sounded a little implausible, I'll admit. But I trusted Manuela and couldn't imagine her stealing anything. Sure, she'd acted strangely when I asked her about all of the petty theft, but there had to be another explanation.

Sadly, the rest of the group didn't share my confidence in the young waitress.

"I wonder if you have my binoculars," Stephanie said, cocking an eyebrow.

"And now my digital camera is missing," George added. "Do you know anything about that, Manuela?"

Manuela's eyes widened as they darted back and forth between the unfriendly faces. She quickly buried her face in her palms.

"That's enough!" I said, putting my arm around Manuela. "George, I'm surprised at you. And Stephanie, I can't imagine that Manuela is our thief."

"But everyone else was away all day," said Stephanie. "Except for you, Nancy!"

"You're forgetting about Lupa," George added.

"My mother was sick with a headache," Manuela insisted. "She stayed home to rest."

"And I was with Manuela almost all afternoon," I said. "There's got to be another explanation."

Manuela started backing away. "Excuse me, I must get back to work. I'm sorry you're all missing things. Please believe that I'm not responsible. And if I find them I will return them immediately. I always do."

She turned and ran off, leaving us all bewildered.

"This is awful," said Bess. "Poor Manuela."

George turned to me. "I'm sorry I lost my temper. Manuela is a nice girl, but it's weird that she found the lens."

"Too true—but I just know that Manuela isn't a thief."

Even as I said this to the group, I couldn't help but be confused by something Manuela had said: *If I find them I'll return them immediately. I always do.* She made it sound as if she had so many opportunities to return things.

Interesting . . .

11

Ruffled Feathers

I have an elderly friend named Ms. Benting, for whom I occasionally do errands. One afternoon I was helping her clean out her basement when I came across a few cages. They were small and rounded at the top, and they had tiny square doors. When I asked about them, Ms. Benting had explained that she used to breed parakeets. As I sat in the lounge describing the cages to the scientists that evening it suddenly occurred to me—the cages we'd spotted in the clearing couldn't be anything other than birdcages! I don't know why I didn't realize it before.

"You're sure about this?" asked Parminder.

"Absolutely," I replied.

Mary twirled a purple lock of hair around one finger. "I wonder why they'd have birdcages."

"Did someone say something about birds?" asked Stephanie, who happened to be walking by. "Because I saw one of those scarlet macaws on the trail today. It was so gorgeous! It didn't drop any feathers, though, which was kind of a bummer. I was hoping to find some to go with my new sarong."

I glanced up. "Bess has a bunch of extras. I'm sure she'd be happy to give you some."

"That would be great," Stephanie replied. "I'll go ask her right now."

Astonished, Parminder sucked in her breath. "Ex-cuse me, Stephanie. Did you say you saw only one bird?"

"Well, as far as I could tell," said Stephanie. "If my binoculars hadn't been stolen, I might have seen more."

"I'm asking because scarlet macaws are always found in pairs," Parminder explained. "They mate for life."

"Like penguins?" asked Stephanie.

Mary nodded. "Exactly."

"Weird," Stephanie said as she headed to the tent area. "Well, I'd better find Bess. I'll see you guys later."

Dan looked over at me. "That's so romantic. Don't you think, Nancy?"

"Huh?" I asked. "Oh, I guess so." In truth, I had

other things on my mind. Once Stephanie was out of earshot, I asked, "Are there many scarlet macaws in the rain forest?"

"Not too many," said Parminder. "Fifteen pairs or so. It's funny, usually I see at least a couple every day, but here our week is almost half over and I haven't spotted any."

"It is odd," Mary agreed.

"Wait a second!" I said as my mind quickly shifted gears. I was ninety-eight percent sure that I'd just stumbled across a clue. Turning to the scientists, I asked, "What happens to birds when they get nervous?"

Mary said, "Well, their natural response is funny. They literally ruffle their feathers. That's where the expression comes from."

"And when they ruffle their feathers, is it possible for some of their feathers to come loose?" I wondered.

"Definitely," said Dan. "Birds lose feathers all the time, but they always shed more if they're in danger or nervous about something."

As Parminder stared at me a small smile tugged at the corners of her mouth. "I think our trusty detective is on to something."

"It's just a theory," I admitted.

"Do tell," said Dan.

After glancing over my shoulder, I leaned in and

lowered my voice. "Well, as we've established, the men we spied cutting down trees in the forest had a pile of birdcages with them. Stephanie said she only saw one scarlet macaw, when normally they're found in pairs, and Bess found a group of scarlet macaw feathers underneath the same tree with the net."

The scientists exchanged puzzled glances. "What does all of this mean?" asked Dan.

"Are scarlet macaws very valuable?" I continued.

"Absolutely," Dan replied. "They've been endangered for years. Zoos and collectors would pay top dollar for them."

"So then aren't they illegal to sell?" I asked. "How can a zoo purchase them?"

"An experienced thief would find a way around that," Mary explained. "It's complicated, but doable. They'll forge documents and records to make it look as if their birds are coming from other legitimate places, rather than the rain forest. I've seen it happen."

Parminder interrupted. "I think I see where you're going with this, but I'm still confused. Why are the men chopping down trees if they're after scarlet macaws? And why was there monkey fur in the net?"

"I don't know for sure," I said, as I thought back to the magazine Jason had been reading in the lounge area—*Exotic Birding*. "But I have a hunch."

Dan stared at me with bright eyes. "Won't the supersleuth fill us in?"

I shook my head. "Not yet, but I'll tell you when I'm sure."

As we left the lounge I pulled Parminder aside so I could tell her what I'd learned. "According to Manuela, Esteban didn't leave voluntarily. He was fired."

Parminder bit her bottom lip. "Well, that makes me feel a little better. But I still wish I knew where he was."

"He could be trying to contact you," I said. "Have you checked your e-mail?"

"I do that every time Jason lets me," Parminder said. "There's also a radio at the lodge but, of course, Jason controls it. If he fired Esteban and is trying to keep it a secret, he wouldn't be so anxious to give me messages from him."

"True," I admitted. "I wonder what Esteban knows. If he was fired for asking so many questions, it must be something."

"You're right, Nancy."

"And I'm pretty certain that I'm close to figuring it all out."

I woke up early the next morning—at the crack of dawn—and slipped out of the tent. I planned on doing some more investigating around the lodge. Since Jason's office was locked and he was nowhere to be found, I went into the kitchen to sniff around. It was so early, Lupa and Manuela hadn't even gotten there to start breakfast. I was about to move on to the lounge, when I heard some faint voices from far away.

Walking carefully toward the noise, I found myself near a small path that wound uphill through some trees.

I followed the path, and a few minutes later I came upon a small cabin made of bamboo. It was surrounded by a low, wooden fence, and since the door was open, I walked on through.

Before knocking, I listened. Two women were speaking, but it sounded like they were disagreeing. There was also another noise—like some sort of animal scrambling across the floor.

When I knocked on the door, the voices became silent, and I heard something that sounded like muffled barking. Then there were whispers and doors slamming. Next someone called out something in Spanish.

"It's Nancy," I called. "Can I come in?"

The door swung open, and I was face-to-face with Manuela, who looked panicked. "*Hola*, Nancy. What brings you to our humble home?"

"I didn't mean to intrude," I said, suddenly embarrassed. "I was just walking by and I heard voices."

The noise started up again, and it sounded so familiar. It seemed to be coming from the closet. "Wait—is that a dog?"

Manuela's eyes widened in fear as she shushed me, pulled me into the house, and then slammed the door closed behind us. "Nancy, can you keep a secret?" she asked.

"Sure," I said. "What's going on?"

Lupa shook her head and muttered something I didn't catch.

Manuela turned to her mother. "It's okay, Mama."

"Okay," Lupa replied. She opened up a bedroom door and walked through. Next I heard her open another door, and a moment later, the cutest little puppy came bounding out. She was a mutt with brown fur and circles around each eye—one white and one black. She jumped up and started licking me with her soft, pink tongue.

I giggled as I bent down to play with her. "She's so adorable!"

"Yes, I think so too," said Manuela. "But Jason does not."

"He's terribly allergic to dogs," Lupa explained. "So he banned them from Corcovado Ecologica. This one is a stray that we took in last month, but we promised to get rid of her."

Manuela went on. "I thought I found her a home

118

a few weeks ago, but it fell through. I've been hiding her here ever since."

"Jason lives far from here, right?" I asked. "What's wrong with keeping a dog at your house?"

"The problem is she's a little too clever," Manuela explained. "She keeps digging holes in the fence and escaping. It's amazing that Jason hasn't caught us. Every time the puppy gets out he has horrible sneezing fits, but for whatever reason, he hasn't made the connection."

"Or he just hasn't said anything yet," said Lupa. "It's very stressful living this way—never knowing if you're going to be the next person fired."

"Horrible. And it stinks that you have to hide her." I bent down to rub the puppy's belly. "What's her name?"

Manuela frowned. "I'm calling her Girl for now. My mom thinks it's a good idea not to give her a real name, because then maybe I won't get too attached."

"It's so hard," Lupa said. "We're trying to find a good home for her, but there's no one around here to adopt her, and we have very little free time to leave the lodge."

"I wish I could help," I said. "Is there anything I can do?"

"Just don't tell Jason," Lupa pleaded. "It would ruin our secret, and our lives. Manuela has told you we're saving for her education, *sí*? I'm homeschooling her for now, but I know that for her to have a successful future, she'll need a university degree."

"I would never tell," I promised. "Your secret is safe with me."

"Thank you, Nancy," said Lupa.

"It's nothing." I backed up toward the door. "Sorry to bug you at home. I was just curious. I didn't mean to be rude."

"It's okay," said Manuela. "We were just getting ready to leave for work."

"Well, I'll get out of your way." Bending down I gave the very rambunctious Girl a final pat.

Now that my ankle was feeling somewhat better, I took a slow walk along the beach, watching waves crash and trying to sort out all the clues I'd found. It stunk how Lupa and Manuela were constantly in fear of losing their jobs—and all over a cute little puppy. It didn't seem fair, but I tried to put this dilemma out of my mind so I could focus on everything else.

I was sure that Jason and the other men from the clearing were birdnapping. Their motive was obviously the money. And I had some evidence: the birding magazine and the cages. I just didn't know how they were doing it, or where the birds were, or what the clearing was for, or even how the missing monkeys fit into the scheme of things. My mind was spinning, but nothing was clicking into place.

An hour later I joined the rest of the group in the dining area.

"Now my hiking boots are missing," said Bess, trudging over to breakfast in her flip-flops.

Stephanie frowned at Kara and Benita. "The bandit strikes again!"

As I approached, Bess shouted, "Nancy Drew! What are you wearing?"

"What now?" I asked, looking down at myself. I was in a plain gray T-shirt and a pair of tan shorts—no fashion emergency as far as I could tell. Then I realized what was on my feet. "Oops!"

I was so distracted, I'd somehow put on Bess's hiking boots—even though hers are purple and mine are green.

"Did you by any chance mistake my binoculars for a necklace?" asked Stephanie hopefully.

"What's that?" I asked, puzzled.

Her friend Benita laughed. "Stephanie has a one-track mind."

"Oh, right . . . your binoculars," I said. "Sorry, Stephanie. No leads yet."

My ankle was still bothering me but I couldn't miss another day in the rain forest, where I hoped to find more clues. So after a quick breakfast, I changed into my own boots, and George, Bess, and I set off.

"I hope we don't have another monkeyless afternoon," Bess said as we climbed the first hill.

"I don't get it," I said, going on to explain what I'd figured out so far, but leaving out my discovery of Manuela and Lupa's temporary pet.

Suddenly Bess put her hand on my arm and gasped. "Nancy, look!"

We'd stumbled across a large tree—and it was filled with monkeys. They were howlers and some had babies on their backs. A few others were eating some sort of wild fruit.

"Amazing!" I gasped.

"I can't believe I don't have my camera," George said. "Look at them all!"

Bess pulled a notebook and pen from her backpack and started counting. "I see eight grown monkeys, plus the two babies—no, three. Does everyone agree?"

I nodded. "Looks that way to me."

We moved on and soon found a troop of capuchins merely a hundred yards away. "Now *this* is how I imagined Costa Rica would be all along," George exclaimed.

"Could you have solved the mystery of the missing monkeys without even realizing it?" asked Bess a few minutes later, when we stumbled across *another* tree filled with even more capuchins.

Don't get me wrong, I was psyched—but I was also confused. This new turn of events was so weird. I couldn't help but be suspicious. "We should check out that clearing again."

"But first we have to finish our hikes," said Bess. "Remember what Parminder said? We must continue with our research—business as usual."

"Maybe we should split up," I suggested. "I can go to the clearing right now."

"No way." George shook her head. "Not after what happened last time."

"George is right," Bess agreed. "We're sticking together."

"Okay, fine," I relented.

Our research took a lot longer because we had to keep stopping to count troops of monkeys. After finishing the Ocean View Trail loop three times, we found a total of twelve groups. I was so perplexed. And we didn't even get a chance to return to the clearing, because the sun was starting to set.

When we got back to camp, we learned that everyone else had the same results that we did. With all of the monkeys back where they were supposed to be, the group was pretty happy.

"This is so great," Benita said. "I was beginning to think I trudged all the way to the rain forest for nothing."

"I think I got some amazing shots," said Bud. "I can't wait to make prints!"

While Parminder admitted to me in private that she was a little wary, this didn't stop her from taking part in the celebration that night.

After a festive meal, we had a big bonfire, toasted marshmallows, and sang songs.

But even stranger than finding a forest mysteriously filled with monkeys was the resort manager's behavior. Suddenly Jason had become the rain forest equivalent of Dr. Jekyll and Mr. Hyde. He was being charming!

He joined us in celebration, and for once he seemed friendly and relaxed—even happy—despite the fact that his eyes were red and watery and he kept sneezing. I worried about Manuela and Lupa. Girl must have gotten loose again.

I handed him a tissue. "You must be coming down with a cold," I said.

"I guess so," said Jason in a stuffed-up voice. He stared up at the sky. "It's such a beautiful night. Look, you can see Orion's belt!"

As everyone else gazed at the constellations in the clear night sky, George looked at me with raised eyebrows. I knew we were wondering the same thing: Why is Jason being so friendly all of the sudden?

As I tried to think of a subtle way to ask, Bess

batted her eyelashes at him and said, "You're in a good mood. Did you win the lottery or something?"

Jason whipped his head around to face her. "Huh? Oh, no." His cheeks flushed red as he smiled even wider.

"So why were you so grumpy when we got here?" George asked bluntly.

"Hey, it's hard running this place," said Jason. "I was so stressed about the missing monkeys and the lack of tourists, you have no idea. Anyway, I'm just glad that everything worked out, and I'm so sorry for how I treated you."

"It's okay," I said. By nature I'm a forgiving person, but Jason's sudden change of personality left me totally confused.

George almost choked on her marshmallow when he asked, "Are you still willing to fix the Web site?"

"I'd be happy to," she said, glancing at me quizzically. "Let's go."

"Oh, I'd prefer to wait until morning," said Jason.

"Are you sure?" asked George.

"Positive." Jason flashed her a strange grin. "I wouldn't want to take you away from the party."

"Okay." George shrugged.

As I watched the orange-yellow flames dance, I wondered if I'd overreacted. If perhaps I'd created the illusion of a mystery when really, there was nothing strange going on. I was about to share this new theory with my friends, but I was interrupted.

It was Dan. He ran toward us, clearly panicked. "My machete," he cried. "Someone stole it!"

12

The Terrible Truth

By the dim light of a flashlight, the rain forest was a whole different universe. Alive and buzzing, its enormous trees cast menacing shadows on our path. Moths and other insects darted back and forth in front of our flashlights, and the various hoots and howls sounding off from every side of the forest made me jump. We pressed on, though.

"I think we're almost there," George finally said in a wary voice. She pushed a prickly thorned branch out of the path and held it back so that Bess and I could pass.

Squinting, Bess waved her hand in front of her face to get rid of a swarm of bugs. "How's your ankle, Nancy?"

"Much better," I said. "It's hardly bothering me at

all." It was a white lie. I'd wrapped my ankle in a brace, and even though it ached with every step, I wasn't going to let anything slow me down.

Since the best way to figure out what was going on at the clearing was to stay by the clearing, George, Bess, and I planned to camp nearby, so that we could get an early jump on the action. We'd crept out of the lodge a couple of hours ago in the middle of the night, after everyone else had gone to sleep. Dan's missing machete and Jason's behavior were both so ominous. I had a feeling something big was about to go down in the clearing—and I wanted to be there for it.

"Hold on a second." George paused as she consulted her GPS.

"We're close, right?" I adjusted the straps on my backpack. It felt so heavy, like someone had filled my sleeping bag with a pile of bricks.

George pressed some buttons, then pointed her flashlight to the left. "It's this way, I think."

"You *think*?" asked Bess.

George shrugged. "I mean, I hope."

Bess sighed. "This awful thought just occurred to me. Remember all of Dan's talk about jaguars?"

"That's just occurred to you?" said George, glancing over her shoulder. "I've been thinking about it for two hours."

Shivers ran up and down my spine. It wasn't the normal tingle of excitement I got when I think I'm on the verge of solving a new mystery. I was nervous. Jaguars would *definitely* slow me down—in a way I *really* didn't want.

Bess asked, "Are you sure this is a good idea, Nan?"

"I never said this was a good idea," I explained. "I said it was the only one I could come up with."

Bess shot me an angry look. It wasn't hard to tell she'd about had it. Then she smirked, and I knew she was still with me.

"Look," said George. "We've made it this far and nothing really bad has happened."

Suddenly a clap of thunder echoed through the air. "Guess I spoke too soon," she said as the raindrops started falling. Groaning, we got into our rain gear and trudged on.

"According to my calculations, we're less than half a mile away," George told us a minute later.

I breathed a sigh of relief. "Great."

When we finally arrived at the clearing we searched for a spot to hide. "We should be close enough so we can hear what's going on," I reasoned, "but far enough away so no one trips over us."

We found a perfect space about thirty yards away, under a large tree and between two thick bushes.

After we quickly pitched our tent, we all climbed in.

"That wasn't so bad," said Bess, pulling out a towel and drying her hair with it.

"What's that noise?" asked George, beaming her flashlight around the tent. "It sounds like it's coming from right outside."

"Everything sounds like it's coming from right outside," Bess pointed out.

It was true, too. When the trees rustled, we didn't know if it was due to the wind or the rain, or some sort of wild creature waiting to pounce. I wondered how I was going to sleep as frogs croaked, grasshoppers chirped, and howler monkeys bellowed from all around. And those were just the identifiable sounds!

"Anyone feel like hearing a ghost story?" asked George, settling into her sleeping bag, and holding her flashlight under her chin so her face turned a creepy shade of orange.

"Please tell me you're kidding," said Bess.

George clicked off her flashlight, saying, "Sorry."

Despite the noise outside and my worries about what tomorrow might bring, exhaustion crept into my bones. I fell asleep almost instantly.

At sunrise a thundering roar woke me up. I scrambled out of my sleeping bag and darted out of the tent.

A helicopter hovered overhead. It was so close to

the ground it created whirlwinds of dust, and the wind shifted so fast and powerfully, it was hard to stand up straight. My hair whipped in my face and I had to squint to keep the dirt from my eyes.

I yelled for my friends, but the helicopter drowned out my voice.

Meanwhile Bess and George stumbled out of the tent and struggled to stand up straight.

"What's going on?" Bess shouted.

"Don't know," George yelled. "But it doesn't look good."

We pushed on against the wind, struggling to make it to the clearing, and finally knelt behind a bush. Peering through my binoculars, I spied Jason and two other men—the same ones who'd chased us through the forest.

The ATVs were back, but that wasn't the worst thing we saw. Next to those ATVs were cages, and they were filled with scarlet macaws—more than I'd ever imagined lived in the rain forest.

"I'm counting thirty," George said. "They must have every pair in the entire national park!"

It made perfect sense. "Those men were cutting down the trees so the helicopter would have a safe place to land," I said, as the helicopter touched down and the pilot cut the engine. "If only I'd realized this sooner!"

"What are we going to do?" asked Bess. "We can't let them get away with this."

She was right. As soon as the cages were loaded onto the helicopter, there'd be nothing we could do. If we were going to save the stunning tropical birds, we had to act fast.

I swallowed the lump that had suddenly formed in my throat. "We need to cause a distraction," I said. "Get ready to run."

"But what about your ankle?" asked Bess. "Are you sure you can handle another chase through the rain forest?"

"I hope so," I answered, taking a deep breath. Before my friends could argue, I stood up and swiftly marched out into the clearing.

"What's going on here?" I yelled.

The men turned around and Jason narrowed his eyes at me. "Well, if it isn't Nancy Drew and her little sidekicks from River Heights! I should have known you'd be here."

"You can't get away with this," I told him.

Jason laughed. "Watch me!" he said before whispering something to the men.

As they ran toward us, we sprinted in the other direction.

"Was this part of your plan?" George asked me, keeping one eye on the men following us.

"Actually, yes," I replied, heading deeper into the forest. "Be sure to stay close!"

The ground was still damp from last night's storm, and I had to focus on not slipping with every step. The men's angry footsteps thumped behind me as I dodged trees and boulders. Recognizing a particularly tall and spindly tree, I yelled, "This way!" and darted left.

The men were gaining ground. They were just a few feet away. Jason had stayed behind, which meant that I didn't have a minute to spare.

I held my breath. We were getting closer. "This path leads to the monkey trap."

"Nancy!" Bess grinned. "Are you thinking what I'm thinking?"

"Yes." I huffed. "Are you with us, George?"

She nodded.

We led the men to the right and then to the left. "Almost there," I called, noticing the wide tree wrapped in snakelike vines and the rock that was shaped like Texas. Now damp, it glistened in the early morning sun. "Five more steps . . . get ready to jump . . . now!"

We quickly leaped from the path.

The men were not so fast. They didn't even realize where they were until it was too late. Moments later I heard a crash and shouts.

"Yes!" I shouted.

We slowed to a stop and circled back around. Peering over the edge of the monkey trap, I broke out into a wide grin. The men had fallen into their own trap! Red-faced and furious, they raised their fists at us and shouted in Spanish. We couldn't understand what they were saying, but it didn't matter. Clearly they wouldn't be escaping anytime soon.

"Good work," said George, giving me a high five.

Bess looked around. "What about Jason?"

"He stayed in the clearing. You two run to camp and get the group," I said. "I'm going to stall him."

"Are you sure?" asked George. "That's so dangerous."

Any potential danger just wasn't on my radar. I had to save those birds. "I'll be fine. Just hurry," I said, taking off before they could protest.

Making my way back to the clearing as fast as possible, I tried to come up with a good tactic for stalling Jason.

When I arrived, he was loading the last few cages onto the helicopter, and the pilot had already started the engine.

I ran toward him and yelled, "Wait!"

Jason turned around. "Wait for what? You're a little too late."

Leaning over, I rested my palms on my knees,

cringing at the pain in my ankle and trying to catch my breath. "Where are you going?"

"Not that it's any of your business," he replied. "But since there's nothing you can do now, I might as well tell you. This helicopter will take me to the international airport in San José. A fleet of jets is waiting at the airport, and the planes are ready to take these birds to buyers in Europe."

I gasped. It was just as Dan and Mary had suspected. "That's horrible." My mind raced to come up with a plan to keep him from getting into the helicopter. "How can you do this?"

"If I told you what they're paying me, you'd understand," said Jason, his eyes widening with greed. "It's unbelievable. More than I could ever earn at Corcovado Ecologica."

"So this is all about money?" I asked. "What about rain forest preservation? What about the endangered scarlet macaws?"

"The birds will be well taken care of," said Jason, rolling his eyes. "And there are still plenty of animals in the rain forest."

As if they understood they were in danger, the birds started squawking and flapping their wings in distress. Feathers flew and swirled through the air, propelled by the wind from the helicopter.

I took a step forward. "What I don't understand is why you trapped the monkeys."

He grinned at me. "They kept messing up the bird traps. They'd either tear the traps apart, eat the bait inside, or get stuck in them."

"So you had to round all of them up?" I asked. "And then you captured the birds?"

"Yes, exactly. I had to find a way to get nearly all of the monkeys in the forest. First we trapped them in the trees, and then we transferred them to underground cages. It wasn't easy, but it was pretty brilliant, don't you think?"

"Sure," I said, wanting to humor him so he'd keep talking. "And you kept tourists away by manipulating the Internet booking system."

"Yes," said Jason. "And if it hadn't been for the monkeys, this would have been done long before the River Heights group arrived. I was worried there for a couple of days. When you and George figured out what I was doing to the computer system, I thought you might catch on."

"We did catch on," I pointed out.

Jason grinned. "Not fast enough."

"We caught your friends," I said. "Those other two men are stuck in an underground monkey trap as we speak."

Jason scoffed. "I don't care about them. If they

were dumb enough to get caught, then they deserve to get in trouble. Anyway, it all just means more profit for me."

"You won't get away with this," I warned him.

"I already have," he stated proudly. "I'm leaving the country."

"I'll tell the authorities," I said, placing my hands on my hips. "And they'll find you. I'll make sure of it."

Jason turned to me and grinned. "Yeah, right. You'll do no such thing."

"Yes, I—"

Suddenly Jason lunged for me and grabbed on to my ponytail. I tried to scream, but I was in too much pain. Dragging me toward the helicopter, Jason shouted, "Silly girl. You'll never get a chance to tell anyone because you'll never see anyone again."

13

Caught!

Jason struggled to pull me onto the helicopter, gripping my hair in one hand and my wrists in his other. But I wasn't going anywhere without a fight. Since my feet were still free, I stomped on his toe and then kicked him in the shins as hard as I could.

"Ow!" Jason shouted, as he let go of my hair and cowered over his leg.

I managed to get one arm free and used my momentum to leap from the helicopter, pulling him along with me. We both tumbled to the ground.

Scrambling to my feet, I started running, but Jason grabbed onto my ankle and jerked it hard, sending me plunging back down.

"Hey you—help me out!" he called to the pilot.

Suddenly the helicopter's engine died down, and the pilot poked his head out the door.

"Grab her!" yelled Jason. He was twice my size and strong, so even though I fought him as hard as I could, he still managed to yank me into a standing position.

"What's going on?" asked the pilot, pulling off his sunglasses and stepping out of the copter. He was a short, stocky man with a dark beard and mustache.

"She's coming with us. You have to help me," Jason ordered.

"I don't have to do anything," said the pilot. "I'm being paid to fly you to San José. No one said anything about kidnapping any girls!"

"If you want to get paid, you'll help me get her on the helicopter," Jason grumbled. "Do you have any rope? I'm going to need to tie her up."

The pilot shook his head. "This doesn't seem right."

"Just do it!" Jason yelled. "I'm not going to hurt her. All I'm doing is stalling her."

"You're already hurting her," the pilot pointed out. "How do I know you're not going to do worse once we're aboveground? No sir, I won't do it. This can't happen in my helicopter."

"If she gets away, we're both going to be in trouble,"

Jason warned him. "She knows me and now she can identify you, too. You know as well as I do that transporting scarlet macaws without the right permits is a major offense. It'll land both of us in jail. Is *that* what you want?"

The pilot looked from Jason to me as he weighed his options.

"Don't do it," I pleaded with him. "Please. You know this is wrong—you just said so."

"I know what I said, but I can't go to jail." As the pilot came closer he glanced at me apologetically. "Excuse me. It's nothing personal."

After a brief tussle, the pilot grabbed my legs, and Jason secured my arms behind my back. I tried to pull myself free, but it was no use. They easily tossed me onto the helicopter, as if I was a sack of potatoes. Then they closed the door, locking me in.

After handing Jason a long length of rope, the pilot sat down at the controls and fired up the engine again.

Was Jason merely trying to stall me, as he had said? Somehow I doubted it. And I obviously had no reason to trust him. Things were looking hopeless, but I continued struggling, my mind racing as I tried to come up with a new escape plan.

The birds squawked loudly, but through the noise I heard something. . . .

"Stop!" someone shouted.

Another voice cried, "You let her go!"

Was it my imagination? As Jason attempted to bind my wrists together, I whipped my head around and looked out the helicopter window.

A huge crowd was descending upon the clearing. Everyone from the lodge was there—Parminder, Dan, and Mary, all of the volunteers, and even Lupa and Manuela. Not only that, they'd brought with them a large police force.

I breathed a sigh of relief. "Um, Jason?" I said.

He gave me a nasty look. "What are you so happy about?"

"Well," I said with a wide grin as I gestured toward the window with my chin, "you kind of have to see for yourself."

Jason looked out. Utterly shocked, he let go of my wrists. I sprang free, opening up the door and leaping from the helicopter.

As soon as my feet hit the ground, I went running over to my friends.

Meanwhile the authorities charged toward Jason and the pilot and quickly placed them under arrest.

With tears streaming down my face, I hugged Bess, George, Parminder, Mary, and Dan. "Thank you all so much!" I cried in a trembling voice. "You got here just in time."

"You're thanking *us*?" Mary asked, incredulous. "Nancy, *we* should be thanking *you*!"

"You just saved the entire scarlet macaw population," Dan exclaimed.

"Not to mention the lodge!" quipped Manuela.

"But if you'd come just thirty seconds later . . . ," I started, thinking about the fate Jason had in store for me.

Bess shuddered, as if she was reading my mind. "Let's not even think about it."

After we released the scarlet macaws into the rain forest, we all hiked back to Corcovado Ecologica. Dan noticed my limp and offered to carry me. It was a totally sweet gesture, but I knew I was strong enough to make it there on my own.

When we were about halfway there, someone tapped me on the shoulder. I turned around to find Parminder, standing next to a handsome and unfamiliar Costa Rican man. He was on the short side, with dark skin and light hazel eyes. "Nancy, I'd like for you to meet someone," she said.

"Wait, let me guess!" I said. "You're Esteban Garcia?"

He nodded. "Indeed."

"I've heard so much about you! It's so great to finally meet you."

"The pleasure is all mine, Nancy Drew." Esteban's voice was soft and deep, and his accent was very slight. "I hear you've been a great comfort to my darling Parminder. I'm just sorry that I helped cause so much stress."

"Yeah, no kidding," I teased. "Where have you been?"

"As soon as I figured out what Jason was doing, I tried to stop him, but he fired me. Since I knew I couldn't stop him alone, I raced to San José. Perhaps it was careless of me, but all I could think about was taking care of the animals in my homeland. I planned to contact Parminder, but I ran into many complications and I lost track of time. It took days for the authorities to take me seriously, and then even longer for them to mobilize and get down here. So long, in fact, that if it hadn't been for you, I would have been too late!"

"I'm thrilled that you struggled so hard to bring an entire police force to the rain forest," I said. "I'm sure that was no easy feat."

Esteban shook his head. "It wasn't, but it doesn't compare to your bravery. Facing Jason and that pilot all alone was so dangerous!"

"It all worked out," I told him. "So how about we agree to share the glory?"

"Okay," said Esteban, his beautiful eyes dancing with delight. "We can both be heroes today."

"Wonderful," said Parminder, giving Esteban a squeeze.

143

She and Esteban held hands for the entire walk back to Corcovado Ecologica. I could tell that they were very much in love. It made me so happy that they were reunited. And it also made me miss Ned, just a little bit. Sure, my time in Costa Rica was turning out to be completely amazing, especially now that I was safe, but I was glad I'd be seeing him in River Heights in just a couple of days.

When we got back to the lodge, everyone was in a festive mood. Someone blared dance music from a portable radio. The volunteers and scientists mingled with the Costa Rican police force in the lounge, joking and laughing, as they recounted the exciting day.

But before I could join the party, I had one last thing to take care of. While Jason and his friends had been caught capturing the monkeys and trying to kidnap the birds, they weren't responsible for the petty thefts at the lodge. That was another, entirely separate matter—but I finally knew what to do about it.

I found Manuela in the kitchen. "We need to talk," I said.

"Okay, Nancy," she replied with a wide smile. "Anything for the hero of the day!"

"Where are they?"

"What do you mean?" asked Manuela, seemingly puzzled.

"You know," I said softly but firmly, leveling my gaze at her. "The stolen goods, the thief—it's time to fess up."

"Oh, that." Manuela lowered her head. "I'm so sorry, Nancy. I don't know what to say. Please don't be mad."

"I'm not mad at all. I just wish you'd said something to me before. Maybe I could've helped."

"I wanted to tell you," said Manuela. "But it was too risky. I knew Jason would fire my mother, and then what? Where would we find work? And how would we save for my education?"

"I know it's been stressful," I told her. "But now it's time to make everything right."

Manuela led me into a small closet off the kitchen and pointed to a cabinet in the corner. I opened it up and found a pair of binoculars, a digital camera, and Dan's machete.

"It's not what you think," said Manuela. "I swear my mother and I did not take these things."

"I know that," I told her. "But it's time you tell everyone else who the real thief is."

14

Another Girl Detective

That night the sunset over the Pacific was truly stunning. As everyone at Corcovado Ecologica enjoyed the view from the lounge, Parminder made a long and flattering toast with her mango juice. It totally wasn't necessary, and was a little embarrassing, but it was kind of nice to hear.

When the applause died down, I stood up and spoke. "I'd like to thank not only Esteban, but the research scientists for their tireless work. And I have some exciting news!" I pulled the stolen goods from my backpack and returned everything to its rightful owner.

"I never thought I'd see these pictures again," George said happily, flipping through the shots stored on her digital camera.

"I don't understand," said Dan. "Where did you find this?"

"Well, you were all right in a sense," I started. "There is a thief at Corcovado Ecologica."

"Was it Jason?" Stephanie wondered.

I shook my head. "It's not a he. It's a *she.*"

"But you insisted that Manuela was innocent," George reminded me.

"Manuela *is* innocent," I said. "But she's been covering up for the real thief."

"It's Lupa?" asked George. "That doesn't seem possible."

Grinning, I shook my head once more. "It's not Lupa, either. Our thief isn't really . . . human."

I called over my shoulder, "Manuela? Lupa? You can come out now."

Manuela marched out of the kitchen with her squirming puppy in her arms.

"Everyone, please meet your thief," Lupa announced a little bashfully. "Her name is Girl!"

Manuela set her puppy loose. Girl's whole body wagged in excitement. She yapped, jumped, and raced around until she'd greeted every single person at the party at least twice.

Even though she wasn't exactly reformed—Bess caught Girl trying to make off with a policeman's baton clutched between her teeth later that night—everyone found room in their hearts to forgive her. She was just a puppy, after all. All she needed was a little attention—and a lot more training!

We spent our final day in Costa Rica repairing all of the damage. There was a ton of work to be done, but we all pitched in. George fixed the Web site as Dan and the sorority sisters picked up all of the trash left in the rain forest by Jason's men. Bud, Cathy, and Mary hiked out to the clearing to plant new trees, and I found and filled in the underground monkey traps with Bess, Parminder, and Esteban.

When we finished with all of that, we got to work on Corcovado Ecologica, fixing broken tents, re-hanging hammocks, cleaning the lounge, and plant-ing new vegetable and herb gardens.

It was a lot of work, and I was exhausted by the time the taxis pulled up to Corcovado Ecologica bright and early on Saturday morning. As the drivers began loading our packs, I noticed something strange. "Wait a minute," I said. "We're missing a bag. Has anyone seen Girl?"

Parminder walked over to the entrance, saying, "It's not what you think! I've decided to stick around for a little while to finish up the research project."

Bess grinned. "That's not the only reason you're staying, is it?"

Parminder blushed as she put her arm around Esteban. "I suppose not," she admitted.

"But you will be back, right?" asked Mary.

"Yes, next week," said Parminder. "But now that Jason is gone, Corcovado Ecologica needs a new manager, so I've been thinking that maybe next year I'll make a big move. After all, someone needs to keep a close eye on things to make sure that nothing like this ever happens again."

George raised her digital camera and pointed it toward the happy couple. "Smile!"

"Are you kidding?" asked Esteban, pulling Parminder closer. "I haven't been able to stop smiling for the past two days!"

After George snapped a couple of shots, I gave the head scientist a hug good-bye, saying, "We'll miss you."

"And I, you," she replied.

Manuela came running over with her puppy on a leash she'd fashioned out of an old vine. "Nancy, guess what? I came up with the perfect name for my dog. It's something I chose to honor my favorite sleuth!"

"Don't tell me you named her Nancy Drew," said George.

"Not quite," Manuela replied. "But close. She will now be called Girl Detective!"

"Girl Detective," I repeated. "I like it."

Before I knew it, we were on our merry—and bumpy—way. Trips home always seem shorter than trips away, and today was no different. I couldn't believe how quickly two hours on the road passed, and suddenly we were at the landing strip and boarding the plane.

I took a seat by the window so I could get one last glimpse of the lush, green rain forest and the winking, blue Pacific.

As the plane took off and gained altitude, Bess sighed. "I can't believe we're heading back home already."

"No kidding," said George. "Before we know it we'll be back in boring old River Heights."

Glancing out the window, I spotted six scarlet macaws gliding over the ocean, right next to our plane. "Look!" I called, pointing to the birds.

"They're following us!" said George.

"It's like they're thanking us for saving them," Bess marveled.

Just then the tropical birds veered off, turning around and heading back over the treetops.

I watched them until I could see just small specks

REDISCOVER THE CLASSIC MYSTERIES OF NANCY DREW

of black moving across the clear sky. Then I turned to George and smiled. "You're right. Before we know it, we'll be back in River Heights," I said. "But somehow I doubt that things will be boring. They never are!"